EMBRACED IN INK

A MONTGOMERY INK: BOULDER NOVEL

CARRIE ANN RYAN

Embraced in Ink
A Montgomery Ink: Colorado Boulder Novel

By
Carrie Ann Ryan

Embraced in Ink
A Montgomery Ink: Boulder Novel
By: Carrie Ann Ryan
© 2020 Carrie Ann Ryan
ISBN: 978-1-947007-83-3

Cover Art by Charity Hendry
Photograph by Jenn LeBlanc

PRAISE FOR CARRIE ANN RYAN

"Carrie Ann Ryan's romances are my newest addiction! The emotion in her books captures me from the very beginning. The hope and healing hold me close until the end. These love stories will simply sweep you away." ~ NYT Bestselling Author Deveny Perry

"Carrie Ann Ryan writes the perfect balance of sweet and heat ensuring every story feeds the soul." - Audrey Carlan, #1 New York Times Bestselling Author

"Carrie Ann Ryan never fails to draw readers in with passion, raw sensuality, and characters that pop off the page. Any book by Carrie Ann is an absolute treat." – New York Times Bestselling Author J. Kenner

"Carrie Ann Ryan knows how to pull your heart-strings and make your pulse pound! Her wonderful Redwood Pack series will draw you in and keep you reading long into the night. I can't wait to see what comes next with the new generation, the Talons. Keep them coming, Carrie Ann!" –Lara Adrian, New York Times bestselling author of CRAVE THE NIGHT

"With snarky humor, sizzling love scenes, and brilliant, imaginative worldbuilding, The Dante's Circle series reads as if Carrie Ann Ryan peeked at my personal wish list!" - NYT Bestselling Author, Larissa Ione

DEDICATION

To Dan.
We made this promise one night. Turns out we never needed it.
I married my best friend far before my thirtieth.
I'm so blessed that we had a decade together.
And when I see you again, we can continue that journey.

ACKNOWLEDGMENTS

Writing this book turned into a passion for hope. I write romance for a living, and yet sometimes I don't feel all that romantic.

Bristol and Marcus changed that for me. At least for the moments we had. And I could never do this alone.

Thank you Chelle for connecting with this book to the point I believed again. You're my best friend for a reason. Also, you need to get Bristol top. You know it.

Thank you Jenn and your team for finding my Marcus! That trip to LA was so much fun and I wish we could do it again.

Thank you Charity for this amazing cover! I don't know how you keep doing it!

Thank you Jessica, Staci, Kerry, Eric, Sarina, and Nana for being my sounding board. I might not talk about what my characters need, but you know what I need, and I'll treasure that always.

And thank you dear readers. These Montgomerys make feel like I'm part of a big family, and you're a huge part of that!

Happy reading, everyone!

~Carrie Ann

EMBRACED IN INK

The Montgomery Ink saga continues with an unforgettable romance where two best friends make a bet that could change their lives forever.

Bristol Montgomery and Marcus Stearn have been best friends for so long, they sometimes forget when they weren't as close as they are now. While friends and family think there's something beneath the surface of their friendship, the two have always been steadfast in their stance on no heated looks or deeper feelings.

The problem? Years ago, they promised each other that if neither of them was married by the time Bristol turned thirty, they'd marry each other.

Even though both have long since decided never to force the other into an arranged marriage, circumstances and sheer stubbornness force them to refuse to back out of their deal.

Now, they're determined to get married—even as dangerous exes and feelings they deny, block their path.

CHAPTER 1

1 0 years ago

Turning twenty was an exercise in futility. You were no longer in your teens, but you still couldn't have a drink to celebrate your birthday.

Not that Bristol Montgomery was actually obeying that teeny tiny little law at the moment.

She sipped her cheap champagne as she looked over the group of friends who had gathered for her party and tried not to grimace.

She didn't actually *like* the taste of champagne, but it was her birthday-slash-going-away-party, and she wanted to be fancy, classy, and the epitome of perfection.

She'd have a Coke later to wash her mouth out.

"Well, how is my baby sister?" Liam asked as he came to her side. He wrapped his arm around her shoulders, and she glanced up at him, grinning. He looked exactly like her other two brothers and cousins, though his eyes were different, looking more like their mother's than the rest of the family.

All the Montgomerys had dark hair and light eyes. The men were all big and built, the women mostly curvy, and her female cousins could probably break a man over their knee if someone dared to hurt their family. Bristol might not be able to do that, but she could try.

"I'm doing fine." She leaned into him. "How are you, Liam?"

"Doing great. Mom knows how to throw a party. Though I am wondering why you have a glass of champagne in your hand when I do believe this is your twentieth birthday, not your twenty-first."

Bristol rolled her eyes. "Mom's the one who poured it for me."

"Ah, yes, the whole you're-allowed-to-have-a-single-drink-on-your-birthday-as-long-as-you're-in-the-house-and-not-driving rule. I remember that." He let out a breath, and she knew he was smiling above her head.

"Just because you're an old man who's allowed to drink now, doesn't mean you can try to lower your voice and pretend you're giving me sage advice and thinking of the old days."

"I'm not old. I'm not even thirty yet." Liam grinned, and she smiled.

"Don't tell Mom that you said thirty was old."

"Considering you're the one who lamented over the fact that you were reaching old age at twenty, I really don't think you have a leg to stand on."

Bristol grimaced. "I was having a bad morning. Plus, the fact that Mom couldn't stop laughing at me as I said it probably meant she didn't take me seriously."

"You're the baby of the family. Of course, they're not going to take you seriously when you lament about your age. They've already been through it all before."

"I am not the baby of the family, thank you very much. Aaron is still a teenager," she said, speaking of their youngest brother. "Where is Aaron?" she asked, looking around for him.

Liam shrugged. "Probably making out with a girl in a closet."

She looked at her big brother and rolled her eyes. "You would think since you're the model and all, you would be the one making out with a girl in a closet. Or a guy."

Liam just smirked, shaking his head. "I don't need to make out with a girl or a guy in my parents' closet. I can rent a hotel room to get out of here. And I won't tell you exactly what we'd be doing." He winked, and she visibly shuddered—like she knew he wanted her to.

"Gross. Don't talk about things like that. I am pure and innocent, and I don't need to hear any of that."

Liam threw his head back and laughed, and she flipped him off.

"I'm the birthday girl, and this is my going-away party, you should be nice to me."

"I'm always nice." He paused. "Are you ready for tomorrow?"

Bristol shrugged, not really knowing if that was the right answer or not. "I want to be okay. Though I'm a little nervous."

"You're supposed to be. This is a big thing."

She looked at her big brother, then leaned into his side and sighed. "I thought you were supposed to help me not stress out about things like this."

"No, I'm supposed to *help* you with the big things. Just like the rest of your big brothers are, and your little brother, and your parents. You've got your BFF to help you feel better."

She looked over at her best friend, Marcus, who was hanging out with his sisters. He turned to glance at her over his shoulder and winked.

She smiled and then looked back at Liam. "Marcus

tells me things honestly, too. None of you guys only try to make me laugh and do your best to make me feel better."

"You're about to enter a world where everybody is going to want a piece of you. They're going to tell you that you're pretty and you're amazing, and then they're going to want something. Maybe not money, maybe not fame, but they're going to want you. And your soul, and your heart. So, you're going to have to keep people around who tell you the truth and tell you exactly how it is."

Fear crawled up her spine, though she kept a smile in place. This was her birthday party mixed with her going-away party. She wasn't going to look scared or worried. Because she was Bristol fucking Montgomery. She wasn't scared of anything.

Lies.

"Well, that's a pep talk."

Liam turned and hugged her tightly. She wrapped her arms around her big brother's waist and held on for dear life.

"I love you, baby sister. And even though we're going into slightly different worlds, I know firsthand what happens when people see you differently. You are a nationally renowned cellist, and you're about to be a world-renowned one. You're going to play for kings and queens and dukes and duchesses. For celebrities and for the high-stakes people of the world. I'm so proud of you. However, if you need me, I will be there in an instant. Because you don't have to do any of this alone. I want you to remember the Montgomery that you are, and know that we are flesh and blood, and all of us will always be here for you."

She wiped away tears, really annoyed with herself for crying. "I cannot believe you made me tear up."

He kissed the top of her head and rubbed her back through the silk of her dress. "I didn't mean to make you cry. In fact, I was going to give you this pep talk tomorrow or even when I saw you next in France or Venice because you know I'm going to visit you as much as I can."

"Really?"

He scowled at her. "Of course, I'm going to visit you. You may be an adult and everything, and you may have a whole team that'll be there for you, but your family will be there for you, too. I love you."

"I love you, too. And thank you. I know that it's not going to be easy, but this is what I've been training for my whole life."

"And you are the best at what you do. I can't wait to see where you go. But remember, if you need anything, we'll be on a plane in the next instant," he promised, pausing. "And so will your best friend."

He glared as he said it, and Bristol just laughed. "You say that as if it's a bad thing that Marcus and I are still best friends after all these years."

"I don't know. The first time you brought that boy home, I thought Dad was going to have a fit."

"I was like six."

"And his baby girl was going off to her bedroom, alone, with a boy."

"To have a tea party."

"Yeah, but that's not what Dad thought."

"Oh, shush."

"I will not shush. I totally remember Dad glowering at Marcus for like the first year."

"Well, now he thinks of Marcus like a son, and Dad's very grateful that Marcus and I are only friends. And the fact that Marcus will always be here when I get back."

Liam raised a brow.

"What? What's that look for?"

"Marcus will be here because his job is here, and he likes being at home. While I know you want to see the world, don't forget him when you're gone."

Shock slid through her, so did an oily feeling that made her want to throw up. "I could never forget him. He's my best friend."

"I know, but you're going to change. You're going to be a different person after this tour."

She didn't like the sound of that. "I hope not too different. I like who I am."

"And we like who you are, too." He frowned into his glass. "Just don't take advantage of the fact that he'll always be here when you come back."

She didn't like this. Not the feeling his words pushed through her, and not what he was getting at. "What are you saying?"

"I don't know what I'm saying," he said and then ran his hands through his hair. The style gave him this beach-boy look with his longer hair, and Bristol could actually see women looking as if they were ready to swoon behind him. The fact that her brother was an internationally famous model that women drooled over might make her a little queasy if she thought about it too hard. Still, she did enjoy the way women stopped whatever they were doing and ran into walls while looking at him.

"I'm not going to take advantage of Marcus. I never have. We're best friends. So, we have each other. I'll always be here for him. If he needs me, I'll drop everything."

"I believe you. And I believe that he would do the same for you. However, this is going to be the longest you guys have ever been apart. I don't want you to get hurt if he changes along the way. Just like you're going to change."

For some reason, her eyes stung, and she blinked away tears. "I don't want to think about that, Liam. Stop it, okay?"

She said the words quickly, and Liam nodded before he hugged her tight to him again. "I'm sorry, I'm thinking about my own friends, I guess. They all want something from me, you know? I don't have what you have with Marcus."

"You want me to kick their asses for you?" she asked, her voice a little hoarse. She didn't want to cry, but she had a feeling she would if she thought about this too long.

Marcus had been her best friend for as long as she could remember, and she didn't like the idea that they might change and go in opposite directions. It wasn't something she had planned for, and she had planned on a lot.

So, she'd have to make something happen. Tell him that she was never going to change and drift from him. She would have to cement something, make it so they couldn't walk away from each other.

She had no idea what that was yet, but her mind whirled, and she did her best to come up with something.

"Another glass of champagne?" Liam asked, his voice low. She knew he had to be worried about her if he was offering her more booze.

She nodded, her gaze off in the distance. Liam murmured something, and then was back in the next instant, a fresh glass of champagne in his hand.

"Don't tell Mom." He kissed her cheek. "I'm sorry I'm an ass."

She shook her head, blinking so she could settle her gaze correctly. "You're not an asshole." She paused. "Okay, you are. Then again, so am I."

Liam laughed.

"However, thank you, you're right. I need to make sure I don't take advantage of Marcus, just like I need to make sure others can't take advantage of me where I'm going."

"I didn't mean to put a damper on your birthday. I'm sorry, babe."

She shook her head, then went up on her toes to kiss him on the cheek. "You're my favorite biggest brother."

Liam laughed. "I don't know. Aaron's getting kind of big."

"But you'll always be the old one."

"I'm going to hit you for that one day, but it's your birthday, so not today."

"Thank you for that. For everything. Now, I need to go find my best friend and make sure he knows that I love him." He raised a single brow, and Bristol knew she blushed. "I didn't mean it like that."

"Just checking."

"Oh, shush." She turned and started making her way towards Marcus, downing the rest of her glass of champagne. She set the flute down on a tray and talked with a few other people on her way. People who wanted to say goodbye—some from work, from school, and from classes. A lot of her friends from high school had shown up, and one of the guys that she played with.

"Hey there, love," Colin said, his British accent far too sexy. "I wanted to wish you a happy birthday."

She swallowed, her eyes wide. "I didn't realize you'd be here," she said, fumbling over her words. She had such a crush on this guy, and between the booze in her system and that accent of his, she was probably going to sound like an idiot.

"Well, I'm going on tour with you, so I thought I'd make sure I was here for your birthday. We can celebrate together when we're in Venice if you'd like." He said the words, and it went straight to her belly. She let out a sigh.

"Okay. Maybe. I, uh, need to go find someone, though. I'll see you later? Tomorrow, right?"

Colin winked at her, and she giggled before heading toward Marcus again. She made her way past a few other people and talked with her instructor, who she was now leaving. She shared a little teary-eyed hug with her. Even though the old woman had scared her to death for the first five years of her training, she would still miss her. Finally, she made her way to the other side of the room.

Marcus's three sisters waved, said happy birthday, and then headed off to their boyfriends, leaving Bristol alone in the corner with Marcus.

"Hey there," he said and opened his arms for her. She went into his embrace easily, sighing. The champagne had gone straight to her head, and she had never had more than half a glass before. She knew she was likely to babble if she weren't careful.

"Hey," she said, sighing the word.

Marcus chuckled, his deep rumble against her ear soothing. He smelled like that new cologne she had bought him for his birthday the week before, and she smiled.

"You smell nice."

He laughed again, and she leaned into the rumble. "Considering you picked it out, I hope I smell nice."

She looked up at him then and just smiled while studying his face. He had such a strong jaw, and eyes that seemed to always know exactly what she was thinking. They were a dark brown and piercing. His skin was a smooth brown that shone under the lights. He had shaved his head recently, but she knew he regretted it. He had spent forever growing it out, but for his birthday the month before, he'd decided to shave it to see what it looked like. He wasn't happy, but she didn't mind. She liked the way he looked no matter what.

After all, he was her best friend. She always felt that way.

"Hey, come out with me," he said, pulling away so he could tug on her arm.

She followed easily, needing a break from all the people. She had loved her birthday bash, and the going-away party it had also turned into. She'd talked with every single person there, even the ones that she didn't know but who had wanted to come anyway. Her parents had gone all out for her, and she would be forever grateful, but she needed a minute to breathe. Marcus always understood what she was feeling, and she loved him for it.

"So, are you ready?" Marcus asked as he stuffed his hands into his pockets. They were standing in the gazebo in the back yard, one that her mom had decorated with sparkly lights but hadn't turned on because she didn't want people everywhere all over the property. Bristol didn't blame her.

"I think so? I'm all packed, and my passport's ready to go, and I'm checked into my flight. It's going to be a really long one."

Marcus nodded, studying her face. "That's not what I'm talking about."

"I know." That sick feeling filled her again, and she swallowed hard. "I wish you could come."

"A cellist doesn't need a librarian. Especially one who's still in school to get their degree."

"I don't know, I'm going to some of the most famous libraries in the world. I'm sure you'd want to visit those."

Marcus laughed. "Yeah, I'll definitely want to go to those, and maybe I'll come out to visit for that. But it's okay, Bristol. We're allowed to have separate lives."

She scowled, not liking the thought of that. "I don't want that. I want things to be the same."

"No, you don't. Like I don't."

"So, you *want* me to go away?" she snapped, getting a little angry. The champagne was wreaking havoc on her emotions.

"That is not what I meant. And you know it. All I want is to make sure you live life to the fullest. And you're going to be amazing. You *are* amazing. I cannot wait to see how high you soar. And I'm going to be here when you need a place to land. I promise."

She looked down at long fingers that made it so she was biologically perfect for playing the cello. She had a few calluses, but her hands were her life. "I don't want to change too much. And I also don't want to lose you."

"You're not going to lose me. They have this thing called a phone. And the internet. It's pretty cool."

She laughed. "But what if you find a new best friend and you stick with them forever? And then you tell them all your secrets."

"You don't know all my secrets," Marcus said, and she scowled.

"I know most of them. Just like you know most of mine."

"I think I know all of them, Bristol Montgomery."

"You're a jerk, but I love you."

"And I love you. And that is why you're allowed to go and fly. I'll be here when you get back."

Tears stung her eyes, and she hated this. She didn't want to leave him. "Let's make a deal. A bet." The idea came to her so quickly, she knew it was likely all the champagne, but she didn't care.

Marcus's brows rose. "Okay. What kind of bet?"

"In ten years, let's make sure that we remain best friends."

"And how are you going to do that?"

She swallowed hard and blurted. "In ten years, if neither of us is married, *we* get married."

Dear God. She'd said it.

He simply blinked at her. "Huh?"

"It's perfect. That way, we will always have each other as our backup plan."

He swallowed hard, and she hoped to hell she hadn't made a huge mistake. "Are you saying that you don't think either of us can get married without each other?"

"I'm not saying that at all." She wasn't sure *what* she was saying.

"So, what *are* you saying?"

"I don't want to lose you. I want to remain best friends."

"Marriage isn't going to fix or ensure that, Bristol."

She let out a breath before beginning to speak quickly. "No, but really... It's a surefire way to make sure we always stay in each other's lives. Because we'll have that bet. And if, in ten years, we're both still single, then we get married."

"You're a lunatic."

"But I'm your lunatic."

That made both of them laugh.

"How much have you had to drink?"

"Not much," she lied.

"So, you're saying in order to make sure we stay best friends, we get married in ten years?"

"Well, it sounds stupid when you say it aloud like that."

"It *is* stupid, Bristol."

"All I'm saying is that you don't want to marry a stranger, right? So, you remain my friend in case we end up having to get married. That way, we make sure we still like each other. We don't want to be a statistic."

Marcus ran his hands over his face and laughed. "Only you would think of this as a way to make sure we stay friends."

"It's because I'm brilliant."

"I'm sure you think so," he said dryly.

"I would flip you off, but we're almost engaged here."

He looked at her then, and they both burst out laughing. "Okay. You know what? Why not?"

Her heart thudded, and she blinked. "Okay?"

"Seriously. Because I have a feeling one or both of us will already be married by then. So, it's probably not even going to matter."

She ignored that thought, though she didn't know why exactly. She just felt like she desperately needed to. "All right, but we have to remain friends so we don't marry strangers. Okay?"

He held out his hand and smiled that heartwarming smile that she knew melted girls' panties from miles away. She never let it get to her, though. Because, after all, he was her best friend.

Maybe her future husband, but she didn't really think it would ever get that far.

"Shake on it," he said.

She put her hands in his but didn't move. "If we shake on it, it's cemented. Because we don't go back on our words or our handshakes or our promises. In ten years, if neither of us is married, *we* get married."

"And you remain my best friend along the way." He paused. "No matter what."

"No matter what." She squeezed his hand, and they shook on it.

She had a feeling that she had just changed the course of her life.

Either that, or she was going to have a really funny story to tell her children about their favorite Uncle Marcus. Because there was no way she was going to marry her best friend.

No way.

CHAPTER 2

*T*oday

Another year and another birthday. Only this time, Marcus Stearn wasn't sure it was merely a birthday. No, tonight could be disastrous. Life-changing. Apocalyptic.

Tonight, he might end up an engaged man.

Why?

Because he was a fucking idiot.

It wasn't as if you could actually blame drinking for the predicament he was in. He'd had a single glass of champagne that night ten years ago. Ten *long* years ago, on a certain woman's birthday, the same woman who had a birthday tonight. A single glass of champagne that had ended in a change of a future. A bet...a promise.

Because, of course, when it came to him and his best

friend, there had to be a dare or a promise that couldn't be broken between them. Not that many people knew that about him and Bristol. It was something they kind of kept to themselves, like the whole idea of the deal.

Ten years ago, they had decided—somehow, in a weird, twisted way of who they were—that if neither of them was married by the time Bristol turned thirty —*tonight*—they would get married.

That was not the stupidest thing in the history of the world, right? More ill-conceived things had to have occurred since then, but he couldn't think of any. And it didn't help that every time he thought of what could happen tonight, he thought of the feelings he refused to allow himself to venture into.

Marcus pinched the bridge of his nose and prayed that she had forgotten.

It had to be a joke, right? They hadn't really mentioned their promise or the event at all over the past ten years. She'd traveled the globe and, sometimes, he went with her for a moment in time. And in all those instances, they'd never mentioned what had been agreed upon, or what would happen beyond this moment.

Oh, in the past few months, he might've noticed that she'd started to look at him differently. If he were honest with himself, he might have looked at her in a way he shouldn't have either, but he hadn't allowed himself to go beyond those blips. He hadn't slept much these past few months. His stress levels had gone through the roof just thinking about what he was going to tell her tonight. What he *should* say.

He didn't know if she still remembered. Surely, she had forgotten. He'd let himself forget over the past decade, even if it had been in the back of his mind every once in a while. He'd been in relationships, as had she, and yet...here they were.

It was only a silly joke, a gamble of faith, and an agreement between friends. People did that in the movies and on TV all the time, and no one ever actually got married after saying that they would be their friend's second choice. That they would somehow rely on each other for marriage. They'd skip the steps of temptation and uncertainty and move on to finding forever—with each other.

He knew Bristol wanted children...just like he did. He knew she wanted someone to be her partner in life because they'd talked about it. And his goals were the same as hers. Happiness, a family...a future.

He couldn't actually add the words *love* or *sex* to that because thinking about having sex with Bristol or loving her in a way that he didn't already love her would make him want to throw up. No, that really wasn't the right thing to think. Because he didn't want to vomit. Not unless it was because of stress.

He thought about Bristol that way...had let himself,

once or twice. How could he help it? She was fucking hot and amazing and sweet, and he was a red-blooded male, who happened to have thoughts every once in a while.

And because he was so damn afraid of losing his best friend, he'd repeated his mantra over and over again. He did not want to have sex with Bristol. He didn't want to love her. Not that he didn't *already* love her, but he didn't want to fall *in* love with her.

Not any more than I already have.

No, he was not going to think about that.

Dear God, now he was thinking himself into circles, and he sounded like Bristol. He let out a breath and tried to focus on the others in the room, only he couldn't, and his mind drifted.

At one point, when she had been with Zia, her ex-girl-friend, he had thought maybe he could get out of the promise made between the two of them. Zia and Bristol had been hot and heavy and had great chemistry. He liked Zia. She and Bristol had been serious enough that he'd thought they were on the path to marriage. Maybe he'd even been a little bit jealous. But that was only because she spent so much time with Zia and not him.

That was the cause of the jealousy.

No other reason.

Then the two had broken up, though they remained friends. And now Zia was off with a man in her life, and happy—possibly getting married.

And now *he* might be getting married.

No. He was *not* getting married.

Bristol had forgotten.

"Why are you growling over in a corner at your best friend's birthday party?" his mother asked as she walked towards him, his father on her arm.

"I'm not doing anything," he said quickly, knowing that was a lie.

"I don't know what your son is doing, Alex. But you need to make sure that he is prepared for this next phase."

Next phase? Did his mother know? Oh, God, had he written what he and Bristol had planned down somewhere, and she had figured it out?

"Old age?" his father asked, grinning, and then winced as his mother punched him in the shoulder. "You know, you still have the same strength you did when you were in college playing softball, love of my life. Come on, Joan." His dad reached around his mother, and when his mother's eyes widened, and she gasped, Marcus tried not to flinch.

He did, however, roll his eyes. "If you two could stop fawning over each other and groping one another for a minute, that would be great."

"Why are you so growly, son?" his mom asked as she moved closer. "Is there something we can do?"

Not in the slightest. Because how could he tell his mother that he might end up engaged tonight because of a promise made between two people who'd vowed to never break their word? Or the fact that he did, in fact, want Bristol. Even if he told himself that he didn't. That he couldn't. "I'm fine. Promise. And what do you mean, prepared?" he asked.

"I was only asking if you're prepared now that you're in your thirties."

"Mom, I've been thirty for over a month." His tone was dry, and when his mother raised a brow, he knew he was right on the edge of getting that *tone* from her. He'd lived on that edge his entire life, even if he was the so-called *quiet* one. He was used to it.

She waved him off. "True, but now that Bristol is thirty, I feel like you're actually in your thirties. Don't give me that look. You're still my baby, but because you guys have always been joined at the hip, now that you're both thirty, it counts." She clapped as she said it, and he snorted.

"It's good to know that Bristol needs to do something in order for it to count for me."

"You know that's not what I mean. I love that little girl like she's my own daughter. It's a shame that you two never actually got together. I would love for her to become a Stearn."

Marcus smiled, shaking his head, even as his stomach clenched. Well, his mother might be getting her wish.

That thought sent shivers down his spine, even as it

warmed him. Hell, he had no idea what to think. And that was the problem, wasn't it?

"Hey there, what are you doing over in the corner?" his eldest sister, Vanessa, asked as she came forward. James, her husband, was right behind her, grinning.

"Yes, are we plotting?" his middle sister, Jennifer, asked, her husband Anthony, right next to her.

"Oh, plotting. Let me help." Andie hopped from foot to foot, her husband, Chris, rolling his eyes behind her.

Every time Marcus looked at Chris, he laughed, because he really did look like one of the Chrises from the *Avengers*. Considering that his sister had had a crush on one of them for a decade and had basically married one? Yeah, that seemed like fate. Fate that made Marcus laugh his ass off, not like the word *fate* that kept creeping into his mind whenever he thought of Bristol.

"Why are we all over here?" he asked, trying to keep calm. The later the hour got, the less likely the whole marriage thing would come up. Other than the fact that his mother had just mentioned it. But she didn't know about the promise. So, as long as they didn't talk about it with Bristol near them, it didn't really exist. And he wouldn't have to turn her down.

Because he was going to have to turn her down, right?

He'd have to break her heart. Or maybe, break his own. Because why would she be brokenhearted? They were friends, after all. Right?

If she actually wanted this, she would have mentioned it. She hadn't, and that meant that they were likely going to ignore it, forget it ever happened. The bet wouldn't matter.

Only, it really did. Because she was his best friend, and even though she had constantly been out of the States and out of the country doing things that she loved, she'd always come back to him.

No matter what separated them, they always came back to each other.

He didn't want to ruin what they had. He couldn't. Only, what if he did?

"Okay, what is up with your face?" Andie asked, and Marcus scowled.

"What's up with *your* face?"

"Hey, that's my wife," Chris said, and Marcus smiled, though he knew it didn't reach his eyes.

"I'm fine, okay? Just tired." That might be the case, mostly because he wasn't sleeping, thanks to Bristol, but it was fine. Everything was going to be *fine.*

"We love you, so if there *is* anything wrong, you need to tell us," his mother said.

"I know that. You guys are great." And that was the understatement of a lifetime.

"And you can't let the Montgomerys adopt you," his father said, his eyes dancing with laughter.

"Although, if they want to adopt all of us, that's okay with us," Vanessa said, grinning.

"Can I be adopted, too?" his mother asked.

"You already know you guys are all honorary Montgomerys, right?" Marcus asked, and the others snorted. "Really? You are. It's sort of a cult situation."

"Did you just call my family a cult?" Bristol asked as she walked forward. Marcus swallowed hard and tried not to think about all the bad things he'd been thinking about recently. Or the dream he'd had the night before. Of Bristol, his fist wrapped around those long, honey-brown locks of hair as he—nope, he wasn't going to think about that.

He did not have sex dreams about his best friend. There were lines, and he did not cross them.

Yet.

"We totally didn't call the Montgomerys a cult," Andie said, pausing for dramatic effect. "But we totally did call you guys a cult," she said primly.

Bristol threw her head back and laughed, a soft, tinkling sound, and she shook her head. She had on long, fancy earrings that he was pretty sure had diamonds in them that shone under the light between the strands of her hair. She had it down tonight, with long waves, and wore a sparkly dress with silver high heels. She looked gorgeous, like a damn princess. And considering that she had played her cello in front of princesses, he could quantifiably make that comparison.

"Yeah, sometimes the Montgomerys feel a little cult-like. But you are one of us." She paused and then grinned. "One of us."

The others laughed, and Marcus smiled, trying to act like everything was natural. Why was this so hard? It shouldn't be. This woman was his best friend—had been forever. Most people would look at them and think they were more than best friends, but they could go fuck themselves. Strangers always thought they were fucking or using each other. But they didn't know Bristol and him. They were always there for each other, and always would be. Even if they accidentally got engaged. Only they weren't going to do that. It wasn't going to happen. It was only a bad bet, like *he* was a bad bet. Not that he actually thought that about himself, but he knew he would be for Bristol. Because she deserved the world, and he was a hometown boy. And he was just fine with that.

"Happy birthday," his mother said, holding Bristol close. Bristol wrapped her arms around his mother and held on tight before hugging the rest of his family, one by one.

"So, how does it feel to be thirty?" Andie asked. "You're no longer a baby. You're now old. Middle-aged." Andie flung her hair back as their mother glowered.

"The next person that mentions anybody in their thirties being old is going to get slapped upside the head. I don't flog, mind you, but seriously, I'll do it."

Everybody backed away, still laughing.

"We're not old, we're no longer babies," Marcus said, holding out his arm. He did it instinctively, and Bristol slid against his side, holding him close in return. He wrapped his arm around her shoulders and squeezed. She felt good, as if she had been there for their entire lives. Even though he had shot up to his height faster, and she had caught up a little, she was still so tiny compared to him.

He didn't know why he kept thinking about things like that. Like how she would feel against him. Because this was simply platonic. Only friendship.

He was delusional.

"Hey there," she said under her breath. He looked at her and let out the breath he hadn't realized he'd been holding.

"Hey there, birthday girl."

"I was beginning to think you and your whole family were going to hide in the corner all night."

"You have so many friends here, we thought we'd let you mingle, have fun, and then come over here where the real party can start when you were ready," his mother said, grinning.

"You know, you are right about that. There are a lot of

people here. But I'm so glad that you guys came. Seriously. You're my second family. And I love you."

His mother wiped tears from her face, and Bristol pulled away from him, hugging his mother close once more.

Marcus tried not to think about the fact that he felt cold now with her warmth gone.

What the hell was wrong with him? He never used to think like this. Oh, there were occasional thoughts every once in a while, but ever since that ticking clock of her birthday came screeching into his ears, the steady pace of what the fuck he was doing became evident, and he couldn't stop the stray thoughts from piling on top of one another until it was all he thought about.

"Okay, enough of that. Now, go chat, and bring Marcus with you. He's been scowling over in the corner for too long."

Bristol narrowed her eyes at him. "I noticed that. I mean, this is my day. I am the center of attention, the princess. And my best friend can't even be bothered to roll out the red carpet or make sure others bow in my presence?"

She grinned, and he rolled his eyes. "You only think you're the center of the universe, Bristol Montgomery."

"My mama told me so, so I totally believe it."

"As your mother should," his mother said. "Now, go, have fun, but make sure you say goodbye before the end of the night. Or if you can't because you're the center of the universe and are busy, just know that we love you. And our gifts are on the table. We can't wait until you come over for dinner."

"I told you not to get me gifts."

"Of course, we did. It's for your birthday," Andie said. "However, we also donated to a charity like you asked us to in the invite."

Marcus smiled and slid his hands into his suit pockets. Bristol did really well in her career. She had albums made, had even been nominated for a Grammy once. She toured the world and was an actual soloist. People begged her to come and play for them.

So, she did really well and was good at saving her money. He made sure of that, as did the rest of her family. She didn't want to blow her earnings on flashy things, even though Bristol loved the shiny. So, her invites had asked for no gifts but said if the guests wanted to do something, they should donate to their favorite charity in her name.

Most people had adhered to that, but not family. Family wanted to do both.

He hadn't gotten her anything. Well, he had, but in retrospect, it was probably a really stupid idea. And it was something he'd made, something that he'd likely never show her. Not when he kept digging himself into a hole.

"Okay, I'm going to go make sure he parties a bit," Bristol said, tugging on his arm. "Come on."

"I'll go wherever you lead me. As always," he said dryly, and his sisters tittered behind him.

He flipped them off, then moved out of the way of his mother's hand. She was really quick, though, and still caught him on the ear.

"Marcus Stearn."

"Sorry, Mom."

She laughed, and he kept his arm around Bristol's waist as they walked from couple to couple and group to group.

"You having fun?" she asked as they made their way around the next couple, a glass of champagne in each of their hands.

A little too reminiscent of ten years before. He sipped slowly, needing a clear head for this.

"I am. But the question is, are you?"

She turned on her heel and looked up at him, her blue eyes wide. "Of course, I'm having a good time. You're here. Everyone's here." She added the last part quickly, and he frowned. He didn't have time to dwell on it though, because she continued. "I love birthdays, but I'm really more of a fan of everyone else's birthdays."

"For someone who is always the center of attention, you sometimes don't like it, do you?"

"Pretty much. But Mom wanted to throw this for me

like she did for my twenties. However, she promised that for my fortieth—*dear God*—we'd go to Vegas for a road trip."

Marcus grinned. "That sounds like a blast."

"Yeah, we'll do a Montgomery road trip for my fortieth, and of course, you'll have to come."

"Because I'm an honorary Montgomery?"

A pause. Then a bright smile. "You know it. Thank you for coming tonight, Marcus. I know you've been a little busy lately."

There was a question in there, but he didn't answer. They hadn't had their regular weekly lunches for the past few weeks, nor had they been hanging out as much as usual. Yes, he had been avoiding her, but he hadn't known what to say.

He really wasn't good at this, and he knew he was ruining it all. But he was really afraid that he was going to fuck things up. And he couldn't. Not when she already meant so much to him. It wasn't like she was really going to want to be with him. It was only a bet. And she had clearly forgotten. She hadn't brought it up yet, in all this time.

Bristol loved teasing him about shit like this. If it really mattered, she would have already been teasing, or maybe would have even gotten down on one knee with a ring at this point. That was who Bristol was. And he fucking loved it.

He just hated the stress right now.

"Happy birthday," he said softly, and Bristol looked up at him, grinning.

"Thank you. Now, I have to start saying my goodbyes to a few people, and my thank yous, but you don't have to hang out with me the whole time."

Marcus shook his head. "No, I'll hang out with you. And I am sorry that I haven't been spending as much time with you recently. I've been busy."

"With that new project?" she asked, and he knew she was honestly interested. Bristol might be the exact opposite of him in some ways, but she loved what he did, just as he loved what she did.

"Yeah, that." He knew it sounded off, but he couldn't help it. While he did have a new project at the library that he was working hard on, that wasn't the reason for his absence of late. No, the reason was all her, but she didn't need to know that.

Not now, not ever.

By the time they said goodbye to everyone, and the Montgomerys started to clean up, Marcus's family and hers were the only ones left, aside from a few stragglers.

He really didn't want to be under the microscope of any of the Montgomerys, considering that Bristol's brothers were big and constantly glared at him recently. He didn't know why. It wasn't as if they knew what his and Bristol's promise to each other entailed. If they did, they'd likely kick his ass. Or try. But it was as if they knew something had changed. At least, on his end. Because Bristol seemed the same.

Didn't she?

"Okay, I think that's it," Bristol said, putting her hands on her hips.

"Head home," her mother said from the side of the room.

"No, I'm going to help clean up."

"The birthday girl doesn't help clean up."

"Yeah, she *makes* the mess," Aaron, her younger brother, said. They flipped each other off while their mother scowled at them both.

"Act like a nice family. The others will learn the truth about us if you don't."

"You know I have a pillow that says something similar to that," his mother said as his family came up.

"I think I have something embroidered that says that, too," Mrs. Montgomery said. Then the mothers began laughing and talking with each other.

His family started to help clean up and mingle with the Montgomerys, and Bristol just leaned back into him, grinning.

"I'm glad our families are friends. It makes everyone so...happy, you know?"

Marcus nodded, barely resisting the urge to kiss her

on the top of the head like he usually did. It somehow felt different now. "Yep. It's a good thing."

Her mother spoke up again. "Now, really, go. Your feet have to be hurting in those heels." Marcus looked down the length of Bristol's body, did his best not to focus on certain curves, and winced.

"Why are you wearing five-inch heels?"

"They were pretty. And my feet are numb."

"Go," the Montgomerys said in unison, and his family agreed.

Marcus tugged on her arm. "Come on, I'll walk you to your car."

"The presents are already in the back, but you don't get to open them until we head to your house tomorrow," her mother shouted.

"I promise. I know the rules."

There hadn't really been a good time for Bristol to sit down and open gifts, so she would do it with her family at her house the next day like they did after large parties like this. He liked the fact that they had little traditions like that. His family tended to just rip into them, but they also didn't have cocktail parties like this one. Not that the Montgomerys did it often, but with some important occasions, sometimes, they did.

He walked her out to her car, sliding his coat over her shoulders as they made their way.

"Thanks. It's not too chilly, but I appreciate it."

"Should've been wearing a coat."

"But I liked the strapless dress. And wearing a coat kind of ruins the lines."

He was not going to think about lines. Except for crossing them. Because, apparently, that's what he was doing.

"By the way, I only had half a glass of champagne, I've been drinking water all night. I knew I wanted to drive home and not stay over."

"To get out of cleaning up?" he asked, laughing.

"No, jerk. Mostly because I like being in my own bed, you know?"

"Sure," he said. He was not going to think about her in her bed. In any bed.

No, he was not.

She let out a sigh and turned to him as they stood in front of her car.

"So," she said.

"So," he echoed. He swallowed hard. "Another birthday."

"Yeah, my thirtieth."

He watched her throat work as she swallowed hard, and he had no idea what to say. What was he supposed to say?

"I guess this means we're engaged, huh?" she asked. His breath caught, his whole body freezing.

"Oh my God. You're engaged?" Andie screamed from

behind them, hopping up and down on her heels. Then she turned around to yell into the house. "They're engaged! Bristol and Marcus are engaged!"

"I knew it! Our babies are getting married! Finally!" his mother shouted before hugging Bristol's mother as the two began to cry.

Marcus tore his gaze from his family and looked down at his best friend. All he could do was blink.

All color had leached from Bristol's face, and she parted her mouth as if she were going to say something, but there really wasn't much to say.

Because people were shouting and clapping, and Marcus knew that things had seriously just gone to hell.

CHAPTER 3

Bristol licked her lips before letting her head roll back, his mouth on her neck. He sucked, licked, and gently used his teeth on her skin. She shivered, sliding her hands down his thick muscles before letting them trail up his back. She sucked in a breath, shook as his hands went down her sides, gripping her hips. Thankfully, they were both naked, so it was easier for them to touch, to kiss. To look and caress. To feel and to *be*.

His mouth traveled down her chest, kissing her breasts, sucking on her nipples. He sucked one peak into his mouth and twisted his tongue the perfect way to send her right over the edge. She came so quickly, it almost felt like a dream. Her legs shook, her body slick with sweat as she tried not to let her thighs spread even wider. She wanted to cling to him, to hold him there. Only he wasn't making it easy, not with her so needy. So ready.

He moved to her other breast and sucked hard, almost to the point of pain, but she didn't care. She wanted more, *demanded* more.

And she was going to get it.

Because he was between her legs fully now, his thick cock pulsating. She wanted his hard length inside her, needed to ride him into oblivion as they both shattered.

She looked up at him and whispered, "Marcus. I need you."

He licked his lips, meeting her gaze before he plunged inside her, so deep, stretching her to the limit. She screamed, the pain exquisite.

Then she woke up.

Bristol blinked open her eyes, her lids heavy with sleep and dreams, her tank top askew so one boob popped out, the other currently being strangled by the rest of her shirt. She licked her suddenly dry lips and looked down to where her hand currently lay, her palm cupping her most delicate flesh.

"Damned traitor," she grumbled. She slowly slid her now damp hand from between her legs and out from inside her panties.

She had once again given herself an orgasm while dreaming. One where her dreams were so real that she'd let herself fully come while asleep, not even knowing her unconscious self couldn't help but keep going.

This wasn't an uncommon occurrence. She'd gotten herself off in her sleep more than once, and had even done so when she was sleeping next to her boyfriend.

He had thought it was hot, and both of them woke up during that instance, and it had led to more sexy times.

Of course, her dream man in that particular dream had been a celebrity she'd had a crush on—one she'd met before and *knew*. So that had been quite embarrassing.

Sex dreams about strangers were usually fine.

After all, you couldn't help where your mind went when you were asleep.

However, the fact that she had met that certain celebrity meant that every time she thought about him, and especially the next time she saw him, she had blushed profusely.

And she hadn't stayed with her boyfriend for long after that. Not because of the sex dream, but mostly because he was a jerk.

Only, hell, now she was having sex dreams about *Marcus*.

Her whole body shook, and she sat up, straightened her tank top, and wiped her hands on her sheets. She would have to wash the damn linens anyway after this.

Only her mind kept going back to the dream. And who starred in said dream.

Marcus. Her best friend.

Her fucking fiancé.

How the hell had that happened?

Running her other hand through her hair, she swallowed hard, wondering if maybe she had drunk too much the night before. No, that wasn't the case. It really couldn't be.

She hadn't had more than a glass of champagne before she accidentally ended up engaged to her best friend.

She honestly hadn't known their bet would go this far. She hadn't let herself think it could. Not when it had been a simple promise between friends that was anything but simple. And though they didn't go back on their promises, *ever*, it wasn't supposed to be real. Only everybody looked so excited, if a bit confused. But they were all super happy. And she didn't want to disappoint them. When Marcus didn't say anything either, she realized there was no turning back. And, boom, engagement.

Now, here she was. Somehow, Marcus had gotten her home, and they hadn't spoken the entire time.

Bristol always talked. She rambled. Constantly.

She'd once rambled to a prince and a duke to the point where they had backed away slowly as if scared.

But with her best friend? The one she'd never once shared a seriously awkward silence with?

She hadn't said a word for the entire fifteen minutes it had taken him to drive to her house.

He had dropped her off, and hadn't said anything either, simply walked her to her door because that's who he was. Neither of them said anything as she closed the door behind herself.

But she knew he was going to be here today.

They would have to talk about it. Fix it.

Somehow.

The doorbell rang twice in a row, and it sounded almost angry.

And then she realized exactly what had woken her up from her naughty dream.

No, it wasn't the orgasm, it was the doorbell.

She jumped out of bed and searched for shorts or pants but couldn't find them.

The doorbell rang again, and then her phone started buzzing. She ran to the door, afraid it was an emergency.

She didn't care that she was only wearing panties and a tank top, and her nipple was showing. She had to make sure everyone was safe.

She flung open the door without bothering to look and froze.

"Marcus," she said. She couldn't help but remember exactly the way her voice had sounded when she breathed his name as he pistoned inside her with that thick and meaty cock.

She did not know what Marcus's cock looked like,

and only Dream Bristol had ever thought about it—*lie*. She was never going to know what his dick looked like.

Right?

Dream Marcus was a totally different thing. He did not exist. She was fine. She wasn't losing her mind.

Bristol looked up at her best friend—or maybe he was her fiancé, she wasn't quite sure right then—and tried to catch her breath.

He had on a leather jacket, a white T-shirt, and jeans. His hands were in his jacket pockets, and he looked at her, his jaw tense.

"Bristol," he growled.

Growled? Marcus didn't growl at her.

And then she remembered what she was wearing. Or rather, what she *wasn't* wearing.

She stumbled back, tripped over her shoe since she hadn't put them away the night before, and nearly fell right on her ass before Marcus reached out and grabbed her by her elbows. He was strong enough to keep her on her feet, and she was grateful.

Because she would've gleefully fallen on her butt, broken a hip, anything to protect her hands and her arms.

They were insured, after all, and needed for her livelihood.

And now she was thinking about injuries to herself

rather than the fact that she was now firmly pressed against her best friend/fiancé—nearly naked.

"I really need to put on some clothes."

"Yeah, I think you really do."

But he didn't let go of her. And she didn't pull away.

Instead, she swallowed hard and looked up at Marcus, and then licked her lips.

She noticed that *he* noticed the action, and she knew they'd both lost their minds. Because that was the only rational explanation for what was going on.

She did not want to have sex with her best friend, but that sex dream, and the way her pussy still clenched at just the thought of him? Okay, maybe she *did* want to have sex with her best friend.

Oh my God, how did this happen?

"You should let go of me," she said softly, and he nodded.

"I don't want you to trip and fall on your ass. You'll never let me live that down if you get hurt because of that."

She scowled. "I wouldn't blame you."

Marcus let her go, and she felt cold immediately.

Again, she didn't want to think about that.

"You would totally blame me. It's what we do."

She nodded, her body threatening to shake. From what? She didn't know. "Okay, you have me there. Now, really, I should go change."

Marcus's gaze slid down her body, and she bit her lip, doing her best not to tug down her tank. Because if she did, trying to cover her panties or her thighs, she'd show all of her boobs rather than the peek of nipple that she was for sure showing already.

Not to mention the fact that her tank top was white, and he could probably see the entire areola. Why did she sleep in this again? She wasn't trying to be sexy, it was simply the fact that she got hot and liked to sleep under like fifty covers.

And now Marcus knew that.

Because every other time he had ever slept over, mostly if they had gotten too drunk or had a sleepover because they were best friends, she'd always worn long shorts or flannel pants, with a shirt that covered her completely. She did not parade herself in front of her best friend.

Until now.

She nodded, turned on her heel, and ran toward the bedroom. She slammed the door behind her and swore she heard a groan from the other room.

It was only in her imagination. Clearly. There was no way he was thinking anything along the same lines she was.

She quickly tugged on jeans, a bra, and a T-shirt. And then pulled on a knit wrap so she could cover herself up even more.

The only thing bare was her feet, and he would just have to deal with that as she hated socks.

She did her best to look calm, but there was nothing settled about her.

Not anymore.

She quickly brushed her teeth, did her business, and tried to make her hair look somewhat presentable, but there was nothing to be done about it.

Later, she would have to do laundry, shower, and try not to think about the fact that the last time she had been in that bed, she had given herself an orgasm. Dreaming about Marcus.

No, she wasn't going to think about that.

It had only taken about five minutes to get everything done, but it felt like an eternity, and yet not nearly long enough.

Bristol took a deep breath and told herself to calm down. She didn't need to stress out. They were going to figure out what to do and tell everybody calmly that they had heard wrong.

And then things would go back to normal.

Whatever her normal was.

She walked out into the kitchen where Marcus stood, her cup of coffee already on the counter and doctored the way she liked it. His cup sat near him as he stood next to the stove, egg whites in a pan along with spinach, cheese, the champagne tomatoes she adored, and turkey bacon.

"That smells amazing," she said honestly, her mouth watering.

Marcus looked over his shoulder and appeared a little relieved.

That she was talking to him? Or that she was actually clothed?

She didn't honestly know what she wanted the answer to be.

"Breakfast is almost ready. Figured you'd need something in your system after last night."

Bristol frowned. "I wasn't drunk."

"Sure."

"I wasn't. I swear." She paused. "Thank you for making breakfast, though. You know that's my favorite meal other than something with strudel and cream cheese and lots of calories."

Marcus huffed.

"Thank you. Really."

"You're welcome. Don't get crabby. Drink your coffee."

"I'm not the one who's crabby," she muttered under her breath before taking a sip of her coffee. It was the ideal temperature and the flavor was spot-on, with the perfect ratio of sugar to cream.

Of course, he got it right. He knew everything about her. He was her best friend.

She held back a wince. Well, he didn't know everything, because if he did, he would know that she'd had a sex dream about him. Now, here he was, watching her. Had practically seen her naked. In the buff, after she'd had really amazing dream sex with him.

How was she going to get through this day without losing her mind?

"I heard that."

It took a moment for her to register what he referred to. Sex? No, not naked dreams. He meant the crabby comment.

"I didn't say it in my head, therefore, I figured you would hear it."

"Eat your breakfast, drink your coffee, and then we'll talk."

Bristol sipped her drink and looked down at the plate that he held out. It was perfectly presented to her, with a little sprig of rosemary on top and everything.

She hadn't even known she had fresh rosemary in her fridge. Marcus had found it and had made it perfect for her.

If he hadn't gone to college to be a librarian, followed something he was passionate about and really damn good at, she'd always thought he would have gone to culinary school.

More tasty goodness for her, though...since he'd always be in her life. That was the reason for the engagement, after all. She wouldn't complain.

Right?

"Thank you," she said, taking the plate from him.

"You're welcome. You could have set the table."

"I just woke up. I'm sorry. Let me have my coffee, and I'll stop being such a bitch."

"Stop calling yourself a bitch. You know I hate when you do that."

She rolled her eyes but smiled. He hated any woman being called a bitch, including if you called yourself one.

She didn't always do a good job of that.

"Seriously, though, thank you for breakfast. I guess we need to talk through the events of last night."

He grunted and started shoveling food into his mouth.

He didn't always eat like that, but she figured it was because he didn't want to talk. Not that she really wanted to talk either. It was already awkward. It was only going to get worse as the day went on.

They finished their meals in silence, another of those awkward silences that she wasn't used to when it came to him. She ate as quickly as he did, drinking a glass of water he had set down on the table for her.

He was always taking care of her. She was doing her best to reciprocate. She wasn't always great at that, though.

It wasn't that she was self-centered. No, she did her

best to take care of everyone, but Marcus always seemed to be two steps ahead of her.

She felt like he had always been in her life. Ever since they were around six years old in the same grade school class and were forced to sit together when the person who had been sharing her desk had pinched her sides and pulled on her pigtails.

She'd kicked the boy in the junk, and Marcus had held her back from doing anything else, mostly because he had wanted to do it himself, but the teacher hadn't said anything about his part.

Instead, Bristol had gotten in trouble and then was forced to sit with Marcus.

They'd become best friends after that, and had rarely been separated since.

Well, not so much in the past ten years. After she had left her twentieth birthday party, an odd agreement in the back of her mind, her life had exploded, her career on a trajectory even she and Liam couldn't fully comprehend.

Her big brother had made it big in the modeling world, and even bigger in the author world, and now she was doing the same in the musical world.

She still couldn't quite believe her luck, even though she knew it wasn't simply luck. She worked long days and would have to work and practice for hours later today for her upcoming tour, as well as to start making new music because she wanted to work on another album.

So, it wasn't only talent and luck.

She worked damn hard.

And Marcus had always been there for her, every step of the way.

She let those thoughts filter through her mind as they finished up their breakfasts, and she took his plate and his mug, doing the dishes without speaking.

"So, what are we going to do?" he asked, and she let out a shaky breath and turned to look at him in her kitchen.

He looked as if he fit there, like he'd always been part of this place. In a sense, he had. He'd helped her move into her house, helped her decide where her spices needed to go in her kitchen. He likely knew he would be doing more cooking here than she would.

He had done so much for her, and it felt like this was a new person standing in front of her now, and she had no idea what to say.

"I don't know what we're going to do."

"We were lying, though... Are we truly engaged?" He voiced the words, and even though she knew he was right, it still hurt to hear them. Did he not *want* to be engaged to her?

It wasn't *that* insane a thought.

She might as well be honest. Because part of her

wanted this. The bit she'd silenced for so long. And if she had this excuse...no, she couldn't think like that. Or, could she?

"I don't know. I mean, that was the rule we set for each other. That we would get married. It happens, right?"

She still couldn't quite believe she'd said those words.

"You want to be engaged?" He didn't sound incredulous. If anything, he sounded neutral, as if he were hiding his emotions. She didn't know why that got to her more than it should.

"I don't know." She ran her hands through her hair and paced around the kitchen. He moved out of the way, and she was grateful because she didn't want to run into him. Didn't want to touch him when that action could suddenly hinder her thoughts. How had that happened so quickly? "I mean, everyone looked so happy. Like they were expecting it."

Marcus nodded. "Everyone assumes we've been secretly dating this whole time. Or forever, however many months it's been."

"Just because they assumed we were dating, which I don't actually believe everyone did, it doesn't mean we actually need to go along with it."

"I know that," she exploded, throwing her hands up into the air. "I'm pretty sure my brothers all knew. I mean, they know everything. The fact that our mothers

looked so happy, as if they had wanted this all this time...
I mean, they couldn't stop hugging each other and crying.
That worries me."

"What do you mean?" he asked, leaning against the
counter. He folded his arms over his chest, and she swallowed hard. She couldn't help it. He had taken off his
jacket, and now his really sexy forearms were on display.
She didn't know when she'd started thinking of his forearms as sexy.

Had it been before the engagement, or was it a new
thing?

Maybe she had just been hiding so much of what she
wanted for so long because of the labels they put on each
other.

Or maybe she was thinking too hard.

"They really think we're engaged," Marcus said softly.

"They do. And I guess we need to tell them the truth.
But your mom, she looked so happy."

Marcus closed his eyes and cursed. "And if we tell her
the truth, she's going to be devastated. You saw the way
she looked."

"I don't want to hurt your mom."

"She's been through enough."

And that was an understatement. Marcus's mother
was an amazing woman but was a heart transplant recip-
ient. And while she was doing well, she was still on many

meds, and her doctors were afraid that her body wasn't going to handle the new heart for very long.

She was strong, but the disease that had wrecked her body the first time could still come back.

Any stress like this would be too much for her, and Bristol felt like a horrible person.

"I don't want your mom to get hurt because of us."

"We can't get married because of my mother," Marcus said, his voice low.

"I know. We also made the rule." She didn't know why she was saying this. Maybe deep down, she did. But she didn't want to think about it right now. "We told ourselves that we would get married once I turned thirty if neither of us was married. And unless one of us is hiding a spouse, we're both single."

"I've never been married, Bristol. Never been close."

She swallowed hard. Zia had been the only person she had ever considered marrying, and in the end, they'd been better as friends.

"I'm single, too."

"So, you want to go through with the bet. Because we made it? And because of my mom."

"Maybe? I think so. I don't want to back out." She said the words quickly, surprising herself.

"You don't."

She let out a slow breath. "I don't think I can. I don't

know... We made that promise for a reason back in the day. Perhaps it was for a good reason."

She had made it because she'd wanted to stay close to Marcus, or maybe there was something more. Honestly, what had she been thinking ten years ago?

Marcus stalked towards her, and she froze, seeing a side of him that she hadn't before. He stood in front of her and then brushed her hair behind her ears before cupping her face with his hands.

"Think about what you're saying, think about what *we're* saying. You want to be my *wife*."

It wasn't a question, but she answered anyway.

"I want to enter this next stage of my life. I want to do it with you. You're my best friend, Marcus. Why not face the rest of our lives together?"

"It's not that easy."

"I don't want your mom to get hurt. I don't want any of our family members to get hurt. We made a promise. Let's stick with it."

He looked down at her and tucked her hair behind her ears again. "Bristol. We're getting married? Seriously?"

Maybe this was all still a dream. Perhaps she was making a horrible mistake. But she nodded, and she saw a look in his eyes, something that maybe made sense.

She couldn't tell.

So, she backed away from him and held out her hand.

"Let's shake on it."

He looked at her hand and snorted.

"You pretty much just asked me to marry you for the sake of my mother, and because we made a promise when we were twenty. And now you want to *shake* on it?"

"Well, why not?"

"This is why not." And then he took another step forward, and his mouth was on hers.

He had kissed her before, of course—quick pecks, busses on the cheek and the top of her head. *Nothing* like this.

She shivered, not knowing what these feelings were bubbling inside her, and sank into him, his tongue brushing along hers once, twice. And then he backed away again, both of them panting, the bare touch of lips not enough.

"Now, *now* it makes a little more sense."

"Sealed with a kiss and all that?"

He shook his head, laughing. "We're probably making a really fucking huge mistake. But you know what, Bristol? Why the fuck not?"

And then he kissed her on the top of the head and left her standing in her kitchen, an engaged woman, and really fucking lost.

CHAPTER 4

*T*hrowing himself mind, body, and soul into work had to help. At least, that's what Marcus told himself. After all, if he buried himself in his job, such as this massive project that he was a little anxious about, then he wouldn't have to think about the fact that he was engaged.

That, somehow, he was going to start a new life with the one person who already knew his soul better than even he did most days.

Maybe this would work itself out and would make sense in the end. Perhaps this wasn't a mistake.

"Why do you look like you're going to be sick?" Ronin —his friend and coworker—asked, as he walked into Marcus's small office, a stack of papers and a leather-bound book tucked safely under one arm. "Because if you're going to be sick, don't do it over the books. We always protect the books. You know the first rule of being a librarian."

Marcus rolled his eyes. "I thought the first rule of being a librarian was to read."

"No, that's what people think it is. It's always to protect the books. And then to protect yourself. While reading. You have to do it all at once."

"You're weird."

"*You're* weird. That's why we're friends."

"Perhaps. Or maybe it's because we've been working here the longest, and I'm all you have."

And odd look passed over Ronin's face, but then he smiled as if nothing had happened. Marcus didn't know a lot about his friend, mostly because Ronin was good at keeping secrets. And that was fine with him. Ronin deserved to have his privacy. And Marcus was good at keeping secrets, too.

Like the fact that his feelings toward Bristol for the past few weeks...months...*years*...might have been burbling in a new direction when he hadn't been looking. Not that he would allow himself to actually say those words aloud. Or maybe it was a good time to do so. After all, she was his fiancée.

Dear God.

"See? You're looking sick again. What's wrong?"

Marcus shook himself out of his reverie. This wasn't

the time to focus on his future—whatever it may be—with Bristol. No, he needed to work. "Nothing. Seriously. Just one of those days."

His family and her family knew that he and Bristol were engaged, but no one else knew outside of those people. Not that that wasn't a lot of people already for an engagement that wasn't fake but *was* sort of arranged in a weird way where he wasn't quite sure how it had happened. He wasn't ready for it to be too real yet. And that meant not telling the world until he was ready.

Only he wasn't sure that he *wasn't* ready.

That inner thought made him cringe, but there was no going back now.

Hell, Bristol was going to be his wife. If they actually went through with this, he didn't know if they were actually going to, but if they did, they were getting *married*. As in telling each other what they were feeling and declaring vows to one another.

And sleeping together.

He froze again, even as Ronin came forward, worry on his face. Fuck. He and Bristol would be sleeping together.

As in…in bed, or out of bed. Either way. They would be together. Flesh to flesh. He would be inside her. Fucking her. Making love. Doing the things married people did.

Oh, hell.

He had kissed her, not on the forehead or the temple or the cheek as usual, but full-on on the lips as if sealing their deal with a kiss. And now he was losing his damn mind.

"Okay, you're going to tell me exactly what's going on, right? 'Cause you're starting to scare me."

Marcus shook his head. "No, don't worry about it. I'm just focused on other things right now, instead of the actual project that we're supposed to be working on."

Ronin stared. "If you're sure." Marcus nodded. "Right, then. The project. I think it's going to be pretty fun. But you're lead on it."

"Well, they came to me, so I'm figuring it out." Marcus was a reference and research librarian, and he specialized in aiding with certain research topics. At the moment, the local university had gotten a huge grant and needed an actual librarian to help on the academic side.

It was a whole slew of research, logging, and other parts of his job that he didn't get to do often these days, mostly because grant funding wasn't the greatest priority for most people at the moment. That meant he spent most of his days researching small grants, but generally bided his time at the desk and in circulation. He loved both parts of his job, but he was really glad to be getting back to the research parts.

Ronin did both on this particular project and worked

closely with him. Although his friend spent a lot of his time on circulation these days.

The library had lost a lot of funding recently, and that meant there were cutbacks, much to the detriment of the library. This wasn't simply a place that collected old books, much like what some politicians thought. Countless people used the library's computers, especially those from areas that didn't have internet. Not everybody was gifted enough to have high-speed broadband, and with schools leaning more towards the technological side of teaching these days and relying heavily on tablets and the internet to get work done, people came in to use the internet and the computers all the time. They used their library for research, to read a book for fiction, nonfiction, anything. Audiobooks, movies, CDs, they had a little bit of everything, and yet not enough of it at the same time.

He loved his job, even when it made his eyes cross. And, with this particular project, he got to work with people, and he got to dive into topics beneath the layers and help with writing a couple of papers. He'd always been a nerd, a geek to some. Had been since he'd been a little boy and picked up his first library card as soon as he could reach the desk. He hadn't been tall enough, but his dad had picked him up, and Marcus had grinned as he signed his name.

He hadn't had big dreams like Bristol, and although

they joked about it, he would rather see the world through a book sometimes, instead of dealing with the idea of traveling in large crowds of people. Bristol was the one who had wanted to see the world. And she *had* seen it. She'd played for kings and queens. For dukes and duchesses.

He held back the growl at the thought of a certain duke who'd gotten a little too handsy. So much so that once he heard about the incident, Marcus had almost bought a damn plane ticket right then, using the funds he had, to fly to London and punch someone in the face. However, he didn't know if that would've ended with him being beheaded or not. Despite being a librarian, he didn't know all the facts and laws when it came to the royals.

Honestly, he'd figured that one of the Montgomerys would get to it first—or Bristol herself. And he knew she would get pissed off at him if he overreacted.

"You don't look sick anymore, but you're looking a little lost. You want to talk about it?" Ronin asked as he leaned against the door again.

"No, I just have some work to do. Do you want to go over a bit of the project since you're going to be working on it with me?"

"I thought you'd never ask." Ronin took a step in and frowned. "If you need to talk about anything, I'm here. I know you have Bristol and some other good friends as well as an amazing family, but you don't have to go it alone. So, let me know if you need to talk about anything. I'm pretty good at things like that."

Marcus smiled softly. "Thanks, man. And I believe you about that."

Ronin grinned. "Good. Now, let's talk data."

Marcus laughed and opened the book, the best sound to his ears.

MARCUS ENDED UP WORKING FOR ANOTHER COUPLE OF hours, about a half-hour past his quitting time, and then unfolded himself from his too-small chair and made his way home. Traffic wasn't too bad, thankfully, because he took the back roads and didn't live in the University area of Boulder. If he had, he might have pulled his hair out. Boulder was growing by leaps and bounds. Hell, the rest of Colorado was, too. Housing prices were insane, and renting was even harder these days. As soon as weed became legal in the state, everyone had moved here, and the housing market went crazy.

Thankfully, Marcus owned his home and wasn't planning on selling anytime soon. If he was just now moving to the city and trying to start a life? He didn't know if he'd be able to afford to live in the state he had been born in.

Shaking his head as he pulled into the garage, he laughed as his mom opened the door to the house.

He turned off his engine and got out, taking his bag with him. "So, apparently, you're making yourself at home, then?" Marcus asked as he made his way up the stairs and kissed his mom on the cheek.

"Of course. You're lucky I didn't bring the Montgomerys with me so we could all have a nice little party." She winked, and guilt slid through him. It wasn't a lie. Because he and Bristol were engaged. Just because he still wasn't sure exactly how that had happened, how it all worked, and what he felt about it, didn't make it untrue.

"One thing at a time, okay?" He did his best to keep his voice calm. He was anything *but* calm.

"Of course, baby," his mother said, patting him on the cheek. "I am making dinner, though, so you're going to have to deal with me."

He grinned. "You're making me dinner in my own house? I kind of like that. Although I did leave out chicken."

"You left out a single chicken breast, and you have vegetables in the fridge. While I understand that it's a very healthy dinner, it's sad that you're doing it all alone. Why isn't Bristol here?"

He looked over his mother's head at his father, who raised his brows. Well, it seemed he *wasn't* going to get a little respite from the interrogation. Not that he blamed them. This had come out of seemingly nowhere.

"Bristol has her own things to do, and it's a workday."

"That's true. It's going to be so exciting when we're all officially a family." She clapped her hands and went into the kitchen, and he looked over at his father, who shook his head.

"She had it in her mind to make her lasagna, but because I can't have as much pasta as I used to, she's making the zucchini version instead."

Marcus's stomach grumbled. "I love the veggie lasagna."

"It's not *that* veggie, there's still ground chicken in it."

"I miss red meat," his father said, rubbing his stomach. "But then, so does your mom." Neither mentioned *why* she didn't eat red meat anymore.

His mom walked back in at that moment. "I miss steak. A really bloody steak. However, ground chicken with zucchini lasagna will have to do. We all know it's my sauce that makes it." She clapped her hands. "Okay now, Marcus, come help me set the table. You can eat and tell me all about your day. And then, maybe, you can tell me the story of how you ended up engaged to your best friend."

Marcus slid his hands into his pockets and looked away from his father.

"I think Bristol needs to be here when I tell the story."

His mother peeked out of the kitchen and frowned.

"Okay. Just know that I'm happy for both of you. I've always known the two of you could do great things together, friends or more. I'm very happy that it looks like you're finally following your heart."

She went back into the kitchen, and Marcus swallowed hard before going to help her set the table.

Was he following his heart? He didn't know.

All he knew was that she had always been part of his life. Since before he could truly remember *not* having her there. She made him smile, made him think. She pushed him. And while that might annoy others, he liked the push. He wasn't too laid-back, but he enjoyed the idea that she knew exactly where she wanted to go, and he could follow if he wished or go in other directions. She never made him do anything he didn't want, and that included saying yes to being with her.

He had to look deep inside and put his feelings in order. If he did that, then he'd make the right choices. They both would. And that was scary. He was afraid that if they looked too hard, he would lose her. He'd already almost lost her once. She had started that new life, and he had been afraid that she would never look back, that she would walk away and become the brightest star she could be. She deserved all of that and more. She had worked her ass off. It had been her hard work, determination, and innate talent that had set her on the stage that she was on now.

When she came to him making that deal, the promise between the two of them, he hadn't been able to say no... hadn't wanted to.

He hadn't wanted to lose her.

Thankfully, at dinner, his mother let him move on to topics such as work and the fact that he probably needed a bigger house. He knew it was because she thought that Bristol was going to move in, but hell, he didn't know. He had no idea what he had gotten himself into, and he needed to figure it out. He just hadn't had the time yet. He had barely slept the night before, and then he'd had to work. He needed to weed through his thoughts and figure out exactly what he was going to do. Marriage was a big thing. So, he needed to determine what he felt for Bristol.

And that wasn't going to be easy.

His parents left, thankfully before his mother did the dishes. He hated when she did them in his house. Not that he wasn't grateful, but his mother shouldn't have to do the dishes, even if she had literally broken into his home to make him dinner.

He used the quiet time after they were gone to think and let his mind wander before he went back into his office and picked up his guitar. There were many reasons he and Bristol were best friends. One of the subtler ones was music. Oh, he was nothing like her in terms of what he could do with music. He had some talent, he liked playing, it was in his blood, after all. His dad could play piano and guitar like nobody's business and even had a band in college.

His dad's old friends still came and played a set or three every once in a while, and they would jam out. He and Bristol join in, with Bristol even playing her cello at times, going with a little rock and blues, something so not like what she usually played.

She would laugh, and Marcus would sing along, loving that she was part of it. Because she was a part of him.

Always had been.

He sat down on his stool and started to strum, just a little melody, something that he used to clear his head. If he continued down this path, he and Bristol would be married.

Did he love her?

Yes. Undoubtedly, yes. She was his best friend, and he loved her. He would do anything for her. They were good together. He had never known anyone like her. Had never had anyone like her in his life.

He hadn't had the type of serious relationship someone his age should have. Not because of Bristol. No, that was never the case. Yeah, some of his girlfriends hadn't liked that he was best friends with a woman, but he never had impure thoughts or whatever the hell you wanted to call it about her when he was with someone. Because that was wrong.

He had always been all in with his relationships, they just hadn't worked out.

While he liked being alone, he didn't like being lonely. There was a difference, and not everybody understood. Bristol always did. Even when she was bossing him around, she still gave him his space.

Not even his sisters did that.

Some of his girlfriends had liked Bristol, had enjoyed being near her, and had ended up being her friend, as well. The only time Bristol had ever judged one of his girlfriends was the one who had only been with him so she could move in. She hadn't wanted to pay rent at her apartment, so she'd figured that she could simply move in and mooch off him. Oh, he had seen beneath the layers of whatever the hell he'd had with her, but Bristol had been the one to lay into him about it.

He hadn't wanted to be lonely, and he *had* liked that woman. In the end, it hadn't worked out. And not because they hadn't liked each other, and not because Bristol hadn't liked her.

He changed chords and started to hum a bit, wondering what he was going to do.

He wasn't going to lazily move into a relationship with Bristol. He also wasn't going to hurt his mother by continually lying. Because it wouldn't be a lie if they kept with it. And if he went in, he'd have to go *all* in. There would be no going back. No tiptoeing around and hurting one another because they were too scared.

After all, he had gone all in with their promise ten years ago. He wouldn't force himself into something that would hurt them both.

Maybe this could work. Perhaps they could have something. Maybe they could be each other's someone.

He loved Bristol. He loved everything about her, even the things that got on his nerves. Because it was her. She was the light of his life, something that he had told his family before, even though his sisters had given him weird looks as his mother beamed.

When his mom had been ill, so sick that he'd thought he'd never see her again, and he had broken down, it had been Bristol he went to. Bristol who held him up.

And when Liam had dealt with his family issues, Bristol had come to him for help. And when Ethan had been hurt, she had come to him then, as well. They were always there for each other, so maybe they could love each other the way others thought they already did.

He didn't know if they could. He'd always told himself that would be stupid. To cross that line would be something they could never come back from. And what would happen if he let himself question that line and let himself feel the temptation he had always buried deep down?

In the end, he didn't know.

What if she deserved better?

What if *he* did?

Or, what if they were exactly what they each deserved?

He didn't know the answers, but as he continued to play, and kept thinking of her, he knew that he didn't want to go back to the way things were before. Sure, that had meant something, and even if he wasn't worried about his mother, something was eating at him. Saying that this could be an excuse.

So, he would go all in.

Even if he had no idea exactly what that meant.

CHAPTER 5

"Oh my God. How is it that I have to hear from your brother that you're engaged?"

Bristol closed her eyes and knew precisely which brother she would have to castrate later.

Of course, it would be Aaron. Oh, her older brothers might pretend that they were all up in her business and like to annoy her. However, this was all Aaron. The one she was closest to in age. Her baby brother. He was always the one meddling in her life. And he also happened to be Zia's friend.

The bastard.

"Hey there, Zia."

"Don't *hey there* me. You got engaged to Marcus. *Your* Marcus. And you didn't even bother to call? To text? To send a pigeon across the pond?"

"I've been a little busy," Bristol said, wincing. She was very thankful that Zia hadn't used video chat, she didn't want to be face-to-face for this. Although her ex-girlfriend—and now friend—was gorgeous, and Bristol didn't mind looking at her, Zia would be able to see every emotion on her face. The fact that Bristol had no idea what she was feeling meant that Zia would know it before she did, and Bristol didn't really want to deal with the ramifications of that particular cascade effect.

"I'm so excited for you! It's about time you married the love of your life. Oh, and I'm totally doing your makeup."

"What?"

Love of my life?

Bristol didn't think that was possible. Was it? She loved Marcus, sure. She wanted him in her life and vice versa forever. But love?

Well, that was the question, wasn't it?

That was why she needed to think, to plan. Because she was going to marry him. And if that kernel of hope within her meant that she loved him more than as a friend, then she needed to think about that.

She wouldn't change their worlds because she hadn't thought about love.

"I'm going to do your makeup. And your hair. I mean, that's a given, right? It would be part of my present to you. I'm not going to actually charge you for it."

Since Zia was a former YouTuber who now had her own makeup line and was doing wonderful and amazing things with her career, the fact that she wanted to do Bristol's makeup was actually quite a nice gift. It was the whole *love of her life* thing that sort of got stuck on Bristol's mind.

Not that she could actually ask Zia what that meant. Oh God, she was doing this all backward. But she couldn't go back now.

Part of her didn't want to, and that meant she had to truly write down her thoughts or something and figure things out.

Because going in circles *clearly* wasn't helping.

"Are you still there? Do I need to fly home? Because I will. Oh, I can't wait for this. You deserve this, baby girl. You and Marcus are amazing."

Bristol shut her eyes and tried to take deep breaths. "You don't need to fly here. Do your thing."

"I *am* loving London." There was something in Zia's voice, but Bristol didn't pry. While Zia might have done so to her, Bristol knew that she needed to go slow with her friend to figure out what was wrong. So, she kept the subject where Zia wanted it: on Bristol.

For now.

"It's a beautiful city. I can't believe you actually live there now."

"It is. I love it here. It breathes creativity, you know? But let's talk about you, Mrs. Future Marcus Stearn."

Bristol licked her lips, suddenly finding them very dry. "Wow, I hadn't actually heard that out loud yet."

Zia laughed, the sound sweet and familiar. When the two of them had dated, they had laughed constantly. They'd ended up better as friends than lovers, but that was fine with Bristol. She needed more friends in her life. She had lost a lot of them over time when she hit a new level of success, and others hadn't quite understood how to deal with that. Asking for money was one thing, expecting it was another. She gave her friends money anyway. She was quite firm on that.

The only person who never really asked her for anything was Marcus. *Her future husband.* Holy hell.

Thoughts of that kiss floated through her mind, and she couldn't help but let out a little sigh.

"I heard that. Are you thinking about him? Oh, I just love this. I always knew the two of you would be perfect for each other."

"What?"

"I told you that. The two of you are great for each other."

"Oh. Yeah, I guess."

"Well, I would hope it's more than a guess. Considering that you're marrying him." Zia paused. "What's wrong? What am I missing?"

"Nothing." Bristol said quickly. "You're not missing anything. Promise."

"Okay. Now I know you're lying."

"I'm not." The fact that Zia could tell she was lying right then and not before didn't really surprise her. After all, Bristol had no idea what she was feeling or thinking, so it technically wasn't a lie. More like an evasion.

She was marrying her best friend, maybe not for the right reasons, but if she let herself believe it, perhaps it would be for the right reasons eventually.

"I'm sorry I didn't call you. Things happened really fast. I wasn't expecting this."

That was an understatement. Or was it? Because it wasn't like the bet had come out of nowhere. It'd been ten years since they made the promise to marry each other. It couldn't be that much out of the blue.

Perhaps he wanted this. Or maybe he didn't want to back down. It was possible he could love her the way she thought she could love him.

"I need to get back to practice, but I promise we'll talk about it later. Okay?"

"Of course." Zia paused. "And you'll tell me what you're feeling? Because you sound like something's off."

"I'm just in practice mode. And I guess things are different. So, I don't really know what I'm thinking."

"Okay. I'm here if you need me. Promise."

Bristol smiled, though Zia couldn't see, then said goodbye before hanging up.

She put her phone on silent, mostly because she needed to focus on practicing, and then went into her office.

Her cello lay there, ready for her, and she rolled her shoulders back before stretching a bit. Her work was hard on her body. She wasn't too small for the cello, but she probably would have had an easier time of it when she was younger if she'd been a couple of inches taller.

She had learned to play, however, and had thrived.

She sat down in her chair and set the cello between her thighs, resting the scroll on her shoulder. She took up the bow, getting her fingers into position, and then she let out a deep breath and slowly slid the bow over the strings.

Music filtered into the air, just a note at a time as she fell into the music, finding her rhythm. There was nothing visual on a cello while playing for her to find the correct notes, there were no frets on the fingerboard. Everything was by ear and touch. But she had long since learned her scales and her notes. They were ingrained in her, like the *Swan* was.

She did her warm-ups and then slowly fell into the music, letting herself flow with the notes.

The first time she had heard Yo-Yo Ma play the cello

when she was a young child, she had cried. She hadn't known why, but it had reached and touched her.

He had played *Cello Suite No. 1 in G Major, Prélude,* and she had fallen in love with music then and there.

Her mother had put her into music lessons because she had asked, even though they were expensive. Her family had been wonderful and focused and found ways to make do. Just like Liam had done with acting, and Ethan with his science and computer camps. Like with the classes Aaron had taken when he was younger, learning how to blow glass by hand in a way that most would never understand.

Each of her family members used their hands in different ways to create. Whether it was through science, math, art, or words. All of her family used their souls to create in some fashion.

She had wanted to be the next Yo-Yo Ma, even though she knew there could only be one.

She'd thrived within his music but had then fallen for Jacqueline du Pré because she had wanted to see a woman holding a cello. She had learned about Beatrice Harrison, and Caroline Dale. She had learned about Sharon Robinson and others.

However, Jacqueline du Pré was the famous player most thought of within her circles when they thought of Yo-Yo Ma. So, Bristol had wanted to be the next Jacqueline and Yo-Yo.

In the end, she was Bristol Montgomery, the new cello player. The cellist.

She let all of those thoughts flow through her even as she filled the room with music. This was *practice*. She had a tour coming up, an album to make, but for now, it was only her and her instrument.

And, of course, it was never just that. Her thoughts lingered on Marcus, because why wouldn't they? He was inside her, always.

She loved her work, she adored performing. But she wasn't a huge fan of stress. And her job brought much stress.

Marcus always seemed to understand that. He'd help her with her stress so she could relax. Whenever he visited her on tour, she knew she'd be able to breathe and focus on what they had, rather than what everybody else wanted from her.

And even as she thought about it, she realized that maybe there had always been something more to their relationship.

Yes, he was her best friend, but was it something more?

She had never allowed herself to think of them as something more in her mind.

She had always thought to put him in a certain box and prove to the world that she didn't have a problem being friends with a man.

That was at least how it had started for her.

Of course, she told herself she hadn't wanted to love Marcus that way. She hadn't let herself think about him sexually. Because that would be wrong. It would prove to the world that men and women couldn't be only friends.

But she had lasted how long? And they hadn't crossed that boundary.

Well, now they sure as hell were. They were *engaged*. They were crossing all kinds of lines. Just his lips on hers alone had changed everything.

And as she faltered on her notes and told herself she needed to rein it back in, she remembered the kiss. And the fact that she wanted another.

The kiss at first had been to seal the deal, to show that they were engaged. And then she'd wanted *more*. Now, they were past it being a promise, a *bet*. They were both far too stubborn to go back on their words now. They were good at being who they were. And now, things were changing. Before, her ex had hated the idea of Marcus and her together, even as friends.

Colin had been an asshole. An egotistical jerk who she actually hated, even though she still worked with him since that's what their careers needed. Each other, apparently.

Colin had loved to insinuate that she was fucking Marcus on the side. But that was fine. Colin had said that she could fuck whoever she wanted, as long as she came home to him.

She should have known that he was just a bunch of hot air—and he was totally cheating on her.

He was an asshole, and she hated him. She didn't like that she'd even wasted her energy on him in the early days of her career. However, their careers were entwined in some respects. And her label even wanted her to do a song with him, not that she wanted to. She didn't really have a choice, contractually, though, and they might have to work together again soon.

She let out a groan and set her bow down before rolling her shoulders back so she could stretch.

Oh, she was going to have to see Colin again. Damn it.

The man who had never understood her relationship with Marcus—not that she really understood it herself now, but that was her prerogative, not her ex's.

Zia had always understood that she and Marcus were nothing more than friends, at least at the time. But the other woman had thought there possibly could be more. The fact that Bristol had always pushed that to the side was her issue. Even now, Zia wasn't too surprised that they were engaged, even though no one had thought they were actually dating. Right? Oh, yeah. There were always laughs and jokes about it, but did anyone *really* think they were dating?

Was this all a farce?

Maybe *she* was the farce.

The doorbell rang, pulling her out of her thoughts, and she felt a clench. What if it was Marcus? What if he was there again? What if there would be kissing? And talking. Then more kissing.

She stood up quickly and made sure her cello was safe before practically running to the door. She was wearing loose yoga pants and a tank top with a sports bra. Not the greatest outfit, but she'd wanted to be loose and comfortable for her practice, and now this is what she'd be wearing when she saw her fiancé.

Oh, dear God, she was engaged to Marcus.

And the more times she said it, the more real it felt. Not like she was playing house. And that meant she was standing there trying to look better, not that Marcus had ever cared about what she wore.

He had seen her in practically everything.

And almost nothing, considering what she had worn when she answered the door the day before.

Then, she supposed, it would be his turn to be completely naked. That was going to be fun.

She froze before she opened the door.

Fun?

Oh, good, now she was thinking of herself having sex with Marcus.

Him plunging inside her as she screamed his name and begged for more.

She squeezed her thighs together and tried to stop thinking of that.

Because if he *was* the one behind the door, this was going to be really embarrassing.

She looked through the peephole and cursed.

No, not Marcus. Though not someone she could ignore either.

She opened the door to Colin.

She knew she shouldn't have thought about him too much. It was like she had conjured him out of thin air.

Say his name three times, and poof, he's suddenly in your house, annoying the fuck out of you like Beetlejuice.

"Hello, Colin," she said, pulling down her yoga top. She didn't want to show him everything. Oh, he had seen it before, but he didn't have a right to now.

"Darling," he said, his crisp British accent annoying the fuck out of her. He leaned down and kissed both her cheeks, and she took a step back.

Of course, that was a mistake, because he took that as an invitation to walk right into her house.

"Wow, you haven't done much with the place, but I love seeing you. It's been a while since we've been near each other, don't you think?" he said.

"Sure," she said. *Not long enough*, she thought, but she knew better than to say that aloud.

"So, what are you doing here, Colin?" she asked, wanting to get back to practice.

And thoughts of Marcus.

"Well, I know our studios have talked about the new tour."

"I'm going on a solo tour."

"And then after, there's talk of the one we're doing together. You know, we are forever entwined."

She held back a gag. She'd even thought that exact thing to herself earlier, but him saying it? No, she was going to be firm with her agent to make sure a co-headliner tour didn't happen. People might want it, but *she* didn't want it. She shouldn't have let herself fall for him for that instant back when she first started, but she wouldn't let herself fall for his kind of traps again.

"No, I have my solo tour, and I don't know what's happening after that." Plus, she was getting married. *Gasp.* Maybe she wanted to spend more time with the person that she would ultimately spend the rest of her life with, and not be across the world working all the time.

"But after that, you're going to need me, darling."

"No, I really don't."

"Whatever. Our agents will talk." He rolled his eyes. She hated that. He brushed her off whenever he didn't like what she was saying. "It doesn't matter. We'll make it work. Because you and I, darling? It doesn't matter that we no longer have one another in our hearts, we will always have one another in our souls."

"I really can't believe you just said that."

"What? Our music breathes life into the world. Without us, it would be a much darker place. Gray without the sun of who we are."

Wow. He was laying it on a little thick today. But that was Colin, after all.

"Now, darling, why don't you greet me the way you used to." She should have known it was coming. She really should have.

One minute she was trying to think of how to get this waxing poet out of her mind and her house, and the next, his lips were on hers, her eyes wide. His tongue slid against hers, invading her mouth, his hands reaching around her. One palm landed on her ass, the other tugged at her hair. She pushed him and tried to bite down, but he kissed even harder.

Colin usually got what he wanted.

And though she didn't let fear creep up her spine, she did let her knee raise just slightly.

And then a voice came from the entryway, and she knew that this was either going to get really bad or be over very quickly.

"What the fuck is going on?" Marcus asked, and Colin froze.

Bristol did, as well.

She really hoped to hell she hadn't just messed everything up. Again.

CHAPTER 6

$\mathcal{M}$arcus swallowed hard and tried to put words to the image running through his head, the sight that was literally right in front of him.

That bastard Colin had his arms around Bristol, his hand threaded through her hair, the other right on her ass.

He'd had his lips on hers as if he had a right to do it. As if he possessed her.

And all Marcus wanted to do was hit somebody for letting that happen.

And because of that feeling, and the rage simmering inside of him, threatening to blow, he held himself back.

Just because he didn't like Colin, didn't mean he had to automatically throw a punch. He had never actually gotten into a fight in his life, and though he wasn't a pacifist, he was damn close sometimes.

Right then, though? All out the fucking window.

Colin and Bristol had a history, he should understand that. It shouldn't enrage him like this.

And he was still figuring out what emotions he felt when it came to his best friend, now fiancée. He shouldn't let all of this jealousy and rage fill him.

Only if he were honest with himself, he had always felt a little jealous when it came to Colin. Because Colin understood Bristol in ways that Marcus never would. Colin had been with her in ways that Marcus never had been.

In ways that Marcus had never allowed himself to think about.

It didn't matter anymore. Bristol was his fiancée, and he'd be damned if he let Colin take advantage or act like he had a right to be here.

To help Marcus along that path, he knew Bristol hated him, too. That thought warmed him more than any form of jealousy ever could.

"Marcus," Bristol gasped as she pulled away from Colin.

Marcus didn't fail to notice that she had to tug a bit harder than she should have to get out of Colin's hold.

"Bristol. I figured now might be a good time to talk. That okay?" A pause. "Colin."

See? His voice was pleasant. He wasn't ready to cut someone. Colin lifted his chin. "Marcus, I didn't realize you'd be by."

Why the hell did Colin need to know anything about what Marcus and Bristol were doing? Asshole. From the way Bristol's eyes narrowed, her thoughts were running along the same lines as his. Good. This fucker needed to leave. Now.

And if he could never kiss Bristol again, that would be fucking fantastic.

"Bristol and I had a few things to talk about. I didn't even know you were in the country."

Bristol's gaze shot back and forth between them, and Marcus did his best not to act like the possessive asshole Colin always came across as.

Because even though Marcus might have a claim, he also wasn't a territorial Neanderthal. At least, that's what he told himself. However, given how Colin's hand was still on Bristol's hip? Well, maybe some of those feelings were starting to come to the surface.

Bristol snorted. "Apparently, he's here because he wants to practice or talk about a tour or something." She rolled her eyes as she came forward, Colin's arm outstretched as if he felt bereft without her touch.

Marcus had an inkling how that particular emotion felt.

"Well, you know a tour would be wonderful for us, darling."

Marcus's brows rose. As far as he understood it, Bristol was done touring with Colin as much as she could. The breakup had ended poorly, and Marcus knew she hated the bastard. However, the asshole had just had his lips on hers.

Maybe he *did* need to hit something.

"I have my own tour coming up. And my own album. I'm a little too busy for anything like that." She let out a breath, then turned. "Hey," she said, leaning into Marcus. He reached out and held her close for a deep hug. They always hugged like this, even before the engagement. Now that they'd taken their next step toward that promise they'd made so long ago, things felt different.

Not that he knew how to deal with that.

"Well, just know that our agents are ready for this. And you know what's best for your career."

Marcus hated the bastard.

"Yes, I know exactly what's good for my career. Anyway, I have to get back to practice. So, what's up, Marcus?"

Marcus didn't like the feeling that he was being pushed out, too, but Bristol's hand was still around his waist, her fingers in his belt loops. Maybe he wasn't being pushed out as much as he thought.

Hell, he hated games. And Colin was all about games.

Marcus and Bristol? Not so much. They were honest with each other. Well, as honest as they could be, considering that Marcus hadn't let himself think about the feelings that he could have for Bristol. Now, they popped into his mind constantly.

He had a right to touch her. Like she had a right to touch him.

Because they were fucking engaged. He still couldn't quite comprehend it, but it was happening. There was no going back now. And, honestly, he didn't want to.

"We have a few things to talk about, so I thought I'd stop by," Marcus said, his voice casual.

"Oh? Do tell."

Marcus seriously hated that British accent.

"Colin, stop being an asshole," Bristol said, and Marcus held back a smile. Because he liked the fact that she stood up for herself. He didn't need to step in for her. And she'd probably kick his ass if he tried. He'd be there if she needed him, though. Like always.

"Asshole? I only want to know. Curious, after all."

Bristol looked up at Marcus and smiled sweetly.

He wasn't sure he liked that expression.

"Colin, my fiancé and I have a few plans to go over. After all, being newly engaged means we have to get a bunch of schedules and details down. But you understand, don't you? You seem to love details."

Marcus's shoulders went back, even as he suppressed

a flinch at the word *fiancé*. Not that he was afraid of the word, it was more that he was surprised.

Colin's gaze went straight to Bristol's hand, and Marcus didn't bother suppressing the wince this time. But he already had that taken care of. At least, he would if his plans went right. Not that he had a real plan when it came to him and Bristol, but he was working on it. Or he hoped so.

"Fiancé? I thought he was just a little friend."

Marcus took a step forward before he even realized what he was doing, his hands clenched at his sides.

Bristol had her hand on his chest in the next instant, putting her body between them. He didn't like that. Oh, he might like the touch, but not the fact that she stood in the line of fire.

"Okay, that's enough. I know you like to be a little sly asshole because you think it gets you all the cookies, but shut up. Marcus is my fiancé and my friend. You acting like a dick isn't going to change that."

Yes, there were many reasons he loved his best friend, and this was only one of them.

"Fine, fine. No need to act all uppity. Congratulations are in order, I guess. I suppose the champagne will be on me the next time we meet."

"Don't count on that being anytime soon," Marcus said, the words gritted through his teeth.

"Touché, I suppose, Mr. Fiancé. Anyway, congratulations. I will be off. I'm sure our agents will be in talks soon. I can't wait to hear more about our tour."

"It's not happening, Colin."

"Aw, you just never know. Now, ta-ta."

He reached out as if to hug Bristol, but she pushed herself closer to Marcus.

Marcus glared at the other man, raising a single eyebrow, and Colin shrugged before walking out of the house.

Marcus quickly shut the door behind him and put both palms on the wood, trying to catch his breath. He closed his eyes, breathed in through his nose and out through his mouth.

He hated the guy, always had. Ever since that birthday party when he had first met the jackass. The one that had changed everything for Marcus. When he'd been so afraid to lose his best friend that he'd made a deal with her that he'd never thought would come to fruition. Because why would she want to marry him? He was a librarian in a big city but didn't tend to leave the area. Bristol got to see the world. And she had seen most of it with Colin.

And there was that jealousy rearing its ugly head again. He never could seem to get out of his own way.

"Marcus?" Bristol's voice was soft as she put her hand on his back. "I'm so sorry about that. I didn't invite him here. I promise. All I wanted to do was practice, and then

Colin showed up and ruined my day, and then he got all growly and jealous even though we haven't been together in years. I want nothing to do with him. I'm sorry he was an asshole to you."

He didn't turn, he couldn't. "Not only to me. He's an asshole to you. Always. I don't know why you have to be near him."

Bristol's hands moved to his back. He felt the warmth through the coolness of his shirt, his skin.

He didn't know how he had cooled, even though it felt as if he were on fire. Was it her touch? The anger? He didn't know. Perhaps he should be worried.

Maybe he was.

"I hate him," Marcus said honestly.

Bristol tapped his back, and he forced himself to turn.

"I hate him, too. But I still have to work with him occasionally."

"I think you're brilliant enough, talented enough, and successful enough that you shouldn't have to."

"Sometimes, I don't have a choice. But, for now, he's gone. And it's just you and me." Her skin pinked, and he wanted to reach out and touch her. So, he did.

He trailed his fingers down her skin, and her tongue reached out and licked her lips. And because he couldn't help himself, he leaned down and brushed his lips against hers. She gasped, and he deepened the kiss, angling her head for more.

He hated that Colin's lips had been on hers. That another man had kissed her, and he didn't know what the fuck to do about it. So, he ignored those thoughts, pushed them from his head, and kissed her again, harder, needier. She moaned into him, her hands sliding up the back of his shirt to rest against his skin. He felt like he was on fire now, her touch igniting the flames. And he kissed, and licked, and bit down on her lip.

He pulled away, his breaths coming in pants, and she looked at him, her eyes wide.

"Hi."

"Hi. I really wanted to do that."

"Oh?" She paused. "Because we need to get used to it?"

He didn't let that hurt him. She was as confused as he was. What were they doing? He didn't know. Because the facade of a fake engagement that wasn't truly fake was only the first layer. There was something between them, something they were doing their best to either ignore or highlight. The fact that they kept going from side to side meant that neither of them knew what they wanted, or what they were doing. But they were still finding their way anyway.

"I think we need to keep doing this. Over time. Just to figure out exactly what we were missing." That was as honest as he could be, and as she gazed at his face and nodded, he figured it was the right thing to say. Either that, or he was simply reaching at this point.

"I'm sorry for Colin."

He shook his head, anger boiling through him. "You don't get to apologize for him. It's not your fault. I just hate the asshole."

"So you said."

"Anyway, now that my friends, family, and Colin know, I suppose this engagement's official. We're heading into this next phase of our lives together. Like we said we would."

He bit down on his tongue so he wouldn't say anything. Mostly because he didn't know what to say, and he didn't want to hurt her. Because he was still trying to figure out exactly how he felt, and along those lines, he needed to figure out what she felt, as well. And even though he knew from his family that the best way for a relationship to thrive was to engage in open and honest communication, that wasn't happening. Not when he didn't know what to say.

"I have something for you," he said instead.

Her brows rose.

"What?"

"Well, it's kind of apropos that Colin looked down at your hand and noticed what was missing when you said we were engaged."

Bristol put her left hand in her right and looked down, her thumb tracing her ring finger.

"It did happen kind of suddenly."

Marcus shook his head. "We had ten years to figure it out. And then we both ignored it for a long enough time that it seemed as if it was out of the blue. But was it?"

He held out his hand, a velvet box in his palm.

Bristol looked down, her eyes blinking rapidly. "Oh. I didn't... I mean, I know. But okay."

He let out a sigh. "Let me do this better." He went down on one knee, and Bristol let out a shocked gasp.

"We don't need to do that. We're already engaged, Marcus. You never have to go down on your knees for me."

His brows rose, and she blushed again.

"Okay, we're going to table that whole image and discussion for a little bit later."

"Yeah, we are. And, I'm going to propose to you the right way. Not just an 'oh, let's do this.'"

"Okay," she breathed.

"Bristol? Will you continue to be my best friend? And move with me into this next phase?"

"I...don't say anything else, okay?"

He frowned. "What?"

"Let's figure out who we are together along this path, but don't make promises or voice feelings that you don't know or feel yet. Like I don't know. Because it's all going too fast, even though I'm the one who made the decision."

"Yeah, I can do that. Because you're still my best friend, Bristol. No matter what."

And then he slipped the ring out of the box and onto her finger. She looked down at the antique setting and smiled.

"I love it."

"I knew you would."

And then he stood up and kissed her again, brushing her hair behind her ear. "We'll figure this out," he said softly.

"As long as you're by my side, we will. Because it's not that I don't want to go into the future alone, it's not that."

"I know."

"I love you, Marcus. I want to make sure that I never hurt you."

He didn't say anything else, and he knew he couldn't. Instead, he lowered his mouth to hers and kissed her again.

They were going about this relationship of theirs completely backward. But the more that he let himself think about it, the more he knew this is what he wanted.

Even if he didn't dare let himself need it too much.

CHAPTER 7

"*I* am getting married," Bristol said, looking directly into her reflection. "I'm not insane."

She snorted at that, realizing that perhaps she was a little crazy. After all, an engagement based on a promise was a bit unconventional. But not completely unheard of.

It could work.

After all, she loved Marcus. She *liked* him. She enjoyed being near him. He was already her best friend.

And if she finally let herself be honest, she was attracted to him. Okay, so that part had already been stated within her mind a few times.

She was hot for her fiancé.

That was good.

She wanted to know what it felt like to have his hands on her, what it would feel like to have him inside her.

She closed her eyes, knowing her cheeks were bright red, and she tried to slow her suddenly quickening breaths.

Before she could get too introspective, the doorbell rang, and Bristol rolled her shoulders back. Today was going to be a good day. Because she was getting to the next step of this whole engagement thing.

The girls were coming over, and they were going to gossip about it.

Thank God. Because she really needed to talk it out.

She slipped her hands down her sundress and made sure her hair looked at least somewhat decent. Then she ran to the front door.

She opened it without looking first and froze.

"Zia?" Bristol asked, her mouth dropping. "You were in London. I told you not to come. Why are you here?"

Her ex-girlfriend and friend sauntered into the room, looking as gorgeous and put-together as ever as she rolled her eyes. "One of my best friends doesn't all of a sudden get engaged to *her* best friend out of nowhere and not think that I'm going to show up."

"I barely followed any of that," Bristol said, laughing.

Zia threw her arms around Bristol's shoulders, hugged her tight, and then kissed her square on the lips. "I missed you, baby girl."

"We're the same age. I'm not your baby girl," Bristol said, hugging Zia tightly. "And you were in London."

"And now, I'm not," Zia said, a sad expression skimming over her face.

"What's wrong?"

"Nothing. I'm fine. However, I am going to be staying in the US for a little while longer."

"Oh, no. Do I need to go beat his butt?"

"You need to do nothing of the kind. All you need to do is tell me exactly what happened, and then tell me all the delicious details about Marcus. I've been waiting to hear them."

"I'm not going to tell you everything."

"Wait? Then why are we here?" Arden asked from the doorway. Bristol laughed.

"Hey, you," Bristol said as she turned toward Liam's woman.

"I'm being serious," Arden said, grinning widely. She was leaning on her cane, one that she didn't always need to use, and Bristol quickly brought the other woman in.

"I'm being serious, too. Do you need to sit down? Are you doing okay?"

"I'm fine. A bad pain day is all. Liam dropped me off, but I wouldn't let him come in and grill you. Mostly because you've been hiding from the family, and I figured there was a good reason."

Zia quickly took the bag of goodies from Arden's hands and introduced herself. "By the way, I'm Zia."

"I've seen photos of you, and Bristol talks about you often. Congratulations on the new line."

"Thank you. And congratulations on landing a Montgomery."

Arden laughed, and Bristol rolled her eyes.

"Oh, shush, you. And, Arden, go sit down. Liam is going to hurt me if I let you tire yourself out too quickly."

"You guys are such fuddy-duddies. I'm fine. I don't even really need the cane today, I rarely do. I just wanted to be sure, and since I didn't bring Jasper along, I didn't have my support."

Jasper was her white Siberian Husky, and the most adorable dog Bristol had ever met.

"You could have brought him over. You know I love him."

"I know, but he and Liam are having a boys' day." Arden rolled her eyes. "I swear that dog is leaving me for Liam. Not that I blame him. I am going to miss him today, though."

"He loves you."

"That is true. Now, I brought over some wine, and makings for a charcuterie board like you asked. We're building them, right? Together?"

"Oh, it's my favorite part. I figured we could all work on it together because I brought some things, and I had a feeling that Holland would, too."

"And speaking of…" Zia said, grinning.

Holland, Ethan and Lincoln's lady love, walked through the door in that instant, her hands full. "I do have the makings for a charcuterie board, and my crockpot is full of balls."

Bristol had to laugh. "Of course, you would think to bring the balls."

Zia winked. "After all, you are a very lucky lady with two sets."

"Okay, that's enough talk about my brother's balls," Bristol said, shuddering.

"Yes, and considering the *other* set of balls belongs to my cousin, let's not talk about that either."

Bristol looked at the other woman by Holland's side and grinned.

"Madison, you came."

The other woman smiled, seeming a little shy. "Thanks for having me. Lincoln said I needed to get out more, and now that he is officially part of the Montgomerys, he said I have a ready-made family waiting for me. Not that I actually want to throw myself into your waiting arms, but it is kind of nice not to only have my family."

"You know, you were always welcome to hang out with us. Even before when Lincoln and Ethan were only friends."

"That's true, but I always felt weird joining in on every single Montgomery gathering."

"There are a lot of those," Holland said. And I'm the newest, so I'm still figuring it out."

"I'm like a minute more into the Montgomery clan than you are," Arden said dryly. "We can figure out our roads together."

"That sounds fine with me," Madison said, and they all laughed.

"Does everyone know Zia?" Bristol asked, herding everyone into the kitchen and making sure Arden sat down. Everyone finished introducing themselves and moved farther into the house.

"Okay, let's get making this charcuterie board as a group, pour some wine, and then we can talk about exactly how the hell Bristol Montgomery is marrying her Marcus."

Everyone looked over at Zia as she smiled and shrugged. "What? I thought we could talk about the elephant in the room. I mean, that is the elephant in the room, right? Are there any more that I'm missing?"

"Not that I know of," Holland said, tapping her chin. "I'm sure we can find more. But first, let's talk about engagements. Because, oh my God. You and Marcus? How did that happen?"

Arden clapped her hands together. "Please tell us. Everything. How long have you guys been dating? When did this happen? I mean, we all thought we saw the chemistry, but we didn't want to overthink it."

"You know, I wasn't even really around as much, and *I* saw the chemistry. I'm so happy for you guys." Madison ran a hand through her hair.

Bristol smiled at her words, even as she broke out in a cold sweat. "Um, let's work on cheese first. Because, yeah, I think I might need some wine, too."

Everyone stared at her and then purposely went back to work, changing the subject to Arden and Liam's next trip on his book tour, rather than the fact that Bristol was finally getting married.

Finally? Oh. That was a word she hadn't meant to use, even in her head. Or was it?

The idea of Marcus and her together sent nervous shivers through her system.

And tempting ones.

Ones she hadn't let herself feel before this.

She pushed those thoughts from her mind, however, because the others would see, and she needed to focus. Everybody got to work, with Madison opening up the wine like a pro. Bristol knew she already liked the woman, but now she had a feeling that Madison was going to be one of her best friends.

Holland and Arden started organizing and laying out the cheese board in a perfectly artful presentation, while Bristol made sure everything was out of the fridge and ready to go.

The meatballs Holland had brought were perfect, mouthwatering, and the ball jokes ensued.

"Seriously, how many ball jokes are you honestly going to make in a day?" Holland asked.

"I don't know, as many as I can fit into my mouth," Zia said, winking before actually putting a meatball into her mouth.

Bristol snorted, wine nearly coming out of her nose, and reached for her water instead. "Okay, that's enough of that."

"Enough of it as in it's now time to tell us everything that happened between you and Marcus?" Arden asked, leaning forward.

"Um. You were there. At my birthday. Marcus and I are getting married. We're going into the next phases of our lives together."

The girls looked at each other and then at her.

"That certainly doesn't tell us much." Arden tilted her head and stared at Bristol. "We won't pry." She paused. "Too deep. Nevertheless, you both look happy, if a little shocked at the outcome. I mean, it did seemingly come out of nowhere, but maybe it didn't. And we're not going to force you to tell us anything."

"Believe me, I've been part of a relationship where everyone had to know everything, and I love the fact that you guys never tried to ask me all the intense questions—and invasive ones," Holland put in.

Zia raised her hand. "I don't mind hearing details about it, though," Zia said, and everyone laughed, the tension mellowing out. "However, we won't talk about the how, mostly because it feels like that's personal," Zia put in.

"But we will be here for you," Madison said, smiling. "Seriously. Marcus is such a nice guy, and I don't know him as well as I know the rest of you, but he always seems to be there for everybody in his circle and outside of it. He has a great job, loves you, and makes you smile. I'm really happy that you guys are making it work."

Bristol smiled even as her cheeks hurt and a cold sensation skated over her. She didn't know what it was, though. Shame? Guilt? No, it couldn't be either of those. Because this wasn't a fake engagement. This wasn't a lie. What it was, was something that was starting at the wrong point of a relationship.

Maybe. Or perhaps she was losing her mind.

"We just knew," she said, hoping that was honest. "It was my birthday, and we looked at each other and... knew. And now, we're getting married."

Everybody sighed, their eyes filling, even though she knew they would have more questions. After all, Bristol had a few of her own. If the roles were reversed, she'd be the one leading the charge, always in everyone's business as she tried to help people into their happily ever afters. But now that it was her? She needed time.

She could kick herself for how pushy she'd been before, even if people had said they appreciated it.

Retrospect and all of that.

"Now, let us see that ring," Zia said. When Bristol held out her hand, she could only smile as the others gushed and squealed, making this dream of hers even more of a reality.

SHE SIPPED AT HER WINE AND TALKED WITH THE GIRLS before everybody headed home, and she was left alone with her thoughts.

She pulled out her phone and dialed Marcus's number without even thinking.

"Hey," she said as he answered.

"Hey."

"The girls just left."

A pause. "I'm still with the guys, though I moved over to another part of the house so they can't hear me. You okay?"

He knew her so damn well. Tears threatened, and she swallowed them back. She wanted to hear his voice. Wanted him near. She was a selfish person, but she couldn't help it. Not when it came to Marcus. Never when it came to him. "I feel like I'm lying even though we aren't. You know?"

Marcus let out a rough chuckle, one that immediately

made her feel like she was on the same page with him. How did he do that with a simple sound? "I feel you. I just think we need to get to know who we are first. You know?"

She relaxed at once, even though hearing his voice did something to her that was not at all relaxing. "Exactly. I haven't changed, neither have you. We're still Bristol and Marcus. We're still the ones who fight and laugh and are dorks with each other. You have always been in my life, and this isn't going to change anything. It's going to cement the fact that we'll always be together."

"I get that."

He paused again, and she frowned even though he couldn't see her. "What's wrong?"

"Do you think it'd be easier if we told everybody what got us here?"

She bit her lip. "It would be easier in one respect, and maybe painful in another. I don't know. I'm not good at this."

"You're good at everything you do, Bristol."

"Haha. We both know that's not true, and I sure as hell don't feel it right now."

"Then let's take that and run with it. You and me. We'll solve this problem of ours."

"What are you saying?"

"Meaning, you and I have had countless dinners together, movie nights, we've gone on trips together, we have literally seen each other around the world, but I've never taken you out on a date. And if we're going to be real about this and find that next path like you keep saying, let's make it work. You and me. A date."

She froze, nervous excitement filling her. "Our first date?"

He cleared his throat. "We're engaged, after all. We might as well figure out what the fuck we're doing."

Laughter bubbled up in her throat. Who knew she could laugh when she had so many other emotions running through her? Marcus, that's who. "Well, that's a good thing to think. Because I don't know what I'm doing."

His voice lowered. "We're getting married, that's the big thing, but maybe that's not the right answer."

She froze. "Getting married is not the right answer?"

"No, that's not what I meant. Getting married is the right answer. Because that's what we want." He paused, and she didn't say anything. She was afraid to.

"So, where are we going on this date?"

"Well, let's figure that out. Shall we? I already know what you like to eat, where you like to go, so...do we want to go somewhere we already love? Or find something new?"

She thought about that, wondering what the right answer was. Because they already had a lot of places they loved, but that was as friends. Were they going to build on what they already had? Or try something new?

Because she was afraid that she wasn't going to give the right answer, she went with what she knew. "Let's go to that Thai place we love."

She could hear the smile in Marcus's voice as he spoke. "The Thai place works. You know I crave their soup."

"And you always get it so spicy it makes both of us cry, but it's the best."

"See? We're already on the right path."

"This was my idea, you know, Marcus? This whole marriage thing. And yet you're the one soothing me. It's always like that."

"It's not. I get stressed out over things, too."

"But I'm the one who blows up. You're always stoic and stern."

"It's my last name, it's what I do."

"Dork."

"I'm a nerd, thank you very much. You would do well to get it right."

She laughed, warmth spreading through her. This was the Marcus she knew and loved. The one she was used to. She wasn't used to the other Marcus. The one that gave her butterflies and made her think about dirty things and warm things that confused her. The one that kissed her and touched her. And made her want more.

There was no holding back now, there was no going back. She didn't want to. Not when the feelings inside her wouldn't go away. She'd hidden them for so long, told herself it would be wrong to want, and yet, here she was.

Near him.

With him.

A temptation encased in passion and trust.

"Have fun with the guys," she said softly after a moment.

"We're starting now, your brothers haven't interrogated me yet, but they will I'm sure."

"Tell them I'll kick their asses if they try.

"No, that's not how it goes. You know my sisters are going to want to interrogate you, too."

She winced, literal fear crawling over her skin. "I know. I'm worried about that."

Marcus laughed. The jerk. "They don't bite. Much. Your brothers, on the other hand?"

"I'll fight them."

"No, I'll fight my own battles. Doesn't matter what anyone else thinks or what they say. You know it's only you and me, right? We're going to do this, find *us*. You and me."

"You and me," she repeated.

After they said goodbye and ended the call, she sat there wondering if she was making another mistake. She was getting good at that. Because this wasn't make-believe, this wasn't playing pretend. This was real life, real feelings, *real*...everything.

And the fact that she was still going through with this meant it wasn't just a facade. She wanted to know exactly what it would feel like to be with Marcus.

And given that she was using this deal and promise as an excuse, that told her that she was far deeper into her own version of *Alice in Wonderland* than she cared to admit.

There was no going back—for either of them.

The parts of her that she tried to ignore were fine with that.

And the rest of her?

That was the question, wasn't it?

arcus ended the call and looked up as Aaron walked into the room. "Was that Bristol?" Aaron asked, leaning against the doorjamb.

They were at Ethan and Lincoln's place, deciding to have a guys' night, although Marcus knew it was mostly so they could interrogate him. He didn't mind. After all, if anyone else had been with Bristol, he would've been in on the interrogation.

And the fact that anger and jealousy slid through him at the thought of anyone else with Bristol meant that he needed to get a handle on his emotions. He knew he'd been having issues when it came to her long before he'd said yes to their engagement, way before he proposed again.

Because he had always wanted her, deep down inside, even if he told himself that he didn't want to.

And that was something he'd have to deal with.

Though he didn't know how.

"Yes, it was Bristol," Marcus said, pulling himself out of his thoughts.

"Well?" Aaron tapped his foot, though thankfully, he looked as if he were exaggerating.

Marcus raised a brow. "What do you mean, well? She's doing fine, the girls just left her place, though I didn't realize they weren't going to stay for long."

"Their thing was earlier, while ours is running later. Although I don't think Holland's coming home directly, so she won't end up hanging out with us at the house. She had a few things to do at her store."

Holland had moved in with Ethan and Lincoln, so technically, this was her place, too. She also owned a fantastically eclectic shop on the main drag of the touristy places in Boulder. She did decently well selling art and knickknacks, and things from local artists, including unique craftsmanship pieces.

He'd bought a couple of items for his house and some gifts over the past few months. In fact, he'd gotten a great piece for his parents' anniversary that he still needed to wrap. He'd probably end up taking it back to the store so Holland could do it better, but he would try, at least.

He frowned. "Ah, I guess I didn't realize that."

"You didn't talk it over with Bristol, then?" There was something in the other man's tone that put Marcus on edge. Aaron was a good man, a better brother, but he was so damn protective that he sometimes reminded Marcus of himself.

And that wasn't always a good thing.

"Is there something you want to ask? Because you sure are acting like you have something on your mind." Marcus might be quiet most of the time, but he also didn't have to take Aaron's shit. He liked Aaron. A lot. The guy was caring, funny, and usually had a quick wit that could make anyone smile, even if they were having the shittiest of days. But he was also as overprotective as the rest of the damn Montgomerys. Like Marcus was when it came to his own family *and* the Montgomerys.

"Why? Is there something you need to say?"

"You're starting to worry me," Aaron said, and Marcus frowned, stuffing his phone into his pocket.

"I am?"

"You're not usually the most talkative of the bunch, but I still can't quite believe that you're dating my sister— no, dating's not the right word. *Engaged to her.* Were you lying to us all this time? Keeping your relationship a secret? I don't know how I feel about that."

And this was why Marcus was still on the fence about telling the truth as to exactly what was going on between him and Bristol. However, it was still his issue to contend with. They needed to work this out between them. Not anyone else. No one needed to know exactly how their relationship had come about. Because it was still in its infancy. They needed to figure it out on their own. And having everybody in their business, trying to get answers from them, wasn't going to help that.

"I know you're her brother and all, but I don't think I need to tell you everything about my relationship with your sister."

Aaron's brows shot up. "You know, I didn't think you'd actually step off like that. I figured you'd be the one to tell us since Bristol is always tight-lipped about her life. However, she *is* my sister, so I do believe you owe me an explanation."

Liam was behind Aaron suddenly and put his hand on Aaron's shoulder. He gave it a squeeze, and Aaron winced. Marcus tried not to find any glee in the action. It mostly worked. "Stop interrogating Marcus. Tonight is guys' night. Meaning, don't be a fucking idiot."

Aaron, however, didn't let up. "I'm just saying, I want to know how you ended up engaged to our baby sister."

"She's *our* baby sister," Ethan said, coming up on Aaron's other side. All the Montgomery guys were pretty much the same size—big, broad, and pure muscle. And considering that most of them worked from desk chairs, Marcus was always surprised by how beefed-up they were. It probably made sense that their guys' night tonight was starting with a workout, and then perhaps a beer if they felt like it.

Ethan and Lincoln had a gym in their basement, and not one with only a single punching bag and maybe a treadmill. No, they had gone all out, considering that Lincoln had a kick-ass job that allowed him to spend money on the two loves of his life even if they didn't always like it that he did.

"Yes, you're the baby," Liam agreed.

Aaron rolled his eyes. "But she's the smallest. I don't like being the baby."

"I don't think your place in the hierarchy of the Montgomerys has changed in the past twenty-something years," Lincoln said, shaking his head.

Marcus grinned and got up from the seat at the desk that he'd been sitting in.

"Considering I'm the baby, too, I feel for you," Marcus said.

Aaron's eyes brightened. "Yes, I always forget that you're the baby. But you have three older sisters."

"They never let me get away with anything, even though my mother always said I was spoiled and coddled."

"See, that makes sense, then," Liam said, squeezing Aaron's shoulder again. "Aaron is spoiled and coddled."

"Fuck all y'all."

"Y'all? We live in Colorado. Not Texas."

"I've been watching westerns. Sue me."

"You know, I was thinking of writing a western thriller," Liam said.

Marcus frowned. "Don't you write one main series where your leading character goes on adventures and almost dies like every other book?"

"I do, but I've had an inkling to write a second series."

"Really?" Marcus grinned, his interest piqued. He loved Liam's work and was a closet fanboy. Not that anyone other than Bristol needed to know his true love for Liam's books.

"I always forget that you're a junkie for his work," Aaron said, laughing.

Marcus shrugged. "Considering I have a Lincoln painting, some of your blown glass, and Ethan built my computer, I'm pretty sure I have a collection of Montgomery creations in my house."

"Well, it's a good thing you're marrying one of us, then," Liam said dryly. "You can finally get that family discount."

"Wait, there's a discount?" Aaron asked, his mouth agape. "You always make me pay for your damn books."

"Hell yeah, I do," Liam said, laughing. "You don't get things for free. Remember, you're already spoiled and coddled."

"I hate you all."

"You love us, but that's fine." Ethan looked over at

Marcus. "Okay, you ready to work out? We're lifting tonight."

"How the hell is this a guys' night? Shouldn't we like... watch sports and eat wings or something?" Aaron grumbled but still looked eager."

"That's next time," Lincoln said dryly. "I don't think we're allowed to gorge ourselves on fried food until after all the weddings so these guys can fit into their tuxes."

"Hey, I'm still the best-looking," Aaron said, sliding his hands down his chest. "Don't you think?"

"No," they all said at the same time, and Aaron flipped them off.

"Seriously, though, we planned on lifting because we needed to get a workout in, and finding time and spotters isn't always easy with our schedules. Next time, it will be wings and junk food and tons of beer." Liam looked around. "Of course, there might be beer after the workout. Just saying."

"Then let's get to it," Marcus said, rolling his shoulders back. "I could punch something, too," he said, wondering why that had come out.

Liam raised a single brow. "If it's because of our precious baby sister, then we're going to need to take you out back and teach you what it means to be married to a Montgomery."

"I have no idea what that means," Marcus said dryly.

Lincoln smiled. "All it means is that they're going to

needle you to death to try and figure out exactly what's going on between the two of you. They're not violent. Thankfully."

"You know, I've been part of this family somehow since I was what, six? And I'm still scared of the Montgomerys."

Lincoln laughed. "I feel you. I might've taken a little bit longer to be part of the Montgomerys, but from the outsider's point of view? It's like a cult."

"One of us. One of us," the three Montgomerys said and then laughed at their joke.

Liam shook his head, a smile playing on his lips. "There has to be another cult that doesn't say that phrase. Right?"

Ethan shrugged. "True, but I'm not really in the mood to be part of the Donner Party."

Marcus laughed. "The Donner Party isn't a cult, is it?"

"As a studier of the occult..." Aaron began and then went off on a tangent about cults, cult leaders, and Kool-Aid.

Marcus pinched the bridge of his nose and made his way down to the basement.

The group did a little lifting, while Marcus also used the punching bag, Aaron being his spotter. They laughed, talked about work, art, and the next game. They pointedly didn't talk about women.

And considering that was usually what they focused on these days, Marcus knew it was because of Bristol.

No one knew exactly what to think when it came to him and Bristol, and considering that he was right there with them, he was glad for the reprieve. "Hey, next time you should bring your friend, Ronin, over," Liam said as they finished up and cleaned the equipment.

Marcus frowned. "Maybe. He doesn't like to go out much."

"Well, we won't force him into working out with us. Maybe when we go out and see a game or something?"

"Yeah, he might like that. He's a good guy, but sometimes, I feel like he hides away in the book stacks."

"You do the same occasionally, but Bristol always brings you out."

Marcus was silent while he waited for Liam to continue, but he didn't.

"You're not going to ask?"

"I don't know if I need to ask anything. I trust my sister, and I trust you."

They were both silent for a moment, and Marcus was grateful that the others were in the kitchen setting up stuff for dinner.

"Nevertheless, if you hurt her, I'll end you. And not only in a book, though that will likely happen, too. We joke that she's our baby sister, but that's the truth. She puts herself out into the world, not simply her music but also her soul, and she needs a safe place to come home to. You've always been that safe place, but if you damage that, if you harm her in any way, her body, her soul, her heart? It's over. I don't know how the two of you started this relationship, but I see the way she looks at you, and the way you look at her. There's something there, so I'm not going to say anything about the fact that we didn't know ahead of time. Because that wasn't for us to know. All I do know is that she's always been yours, just like you've always been hers. So, don't fuck it up."

Marcus swallowed hard.

"She's my best friend, Liam," Marcus said—it was the only thing he could.

"I know. Like Arden's mine."

The others walked into the room at that moment, and they didn't need to say anything else. Marcus picked up his glass of water instead of the beer that he wasn't in the mood for anymore, and then they went back to talking about sports. Of course, as soon as they did, Ethan spoke up.

"Okay, I heard part of what Liam was saying, but I'm going to talk now, too," the other man said, and Lincoln pinched the bridge of his nose.

"Oh God, please don't."

"Don't worry, love of my life, I'm not an asshole."

Aaron coughed into his fist, and Ethan flipped his brother off.

"All I'm going to say is, welcome to the family." Ethan held up his glass, and Marcus swallowed hard, giving the other men a nod.

"Thanks."

"And if you fuck with our sister, we'll fuck with you."

Marcus burst out laughing with the rest of them because Ethan looked so sweet and innocent as he said the words.

Lincoln groaned and covered his face with his hands. "Seriously?" he mumbled into his palms.

"Seriously."

"You guys weren't this bad to me when I joined," Lincoln said, lowering his hands.

"But you were taking Ethan off their hands. Bristol is their precious baby sister, remember?" Marcus said dead-pan, and Ethan's mouth dropped.

"I can't believe you said that," Ethan said and then burst out laughing with the rest of them.

Aaron looked between them, shaking his head. "You know, I might be the youngest, but I didn't think I'd be the last one standing."

Marcus frowned. "What do you mean?"

"The last single Montgomery. I mean, what is Boulder going to do without us? I guess I'm just going to have to carry the load and make sure that everyone knows that there is still a young, sexy, Montgomery left in waiting."

Marcus snorted. "I'm pretty sure everybody always knew you were always available."

"I don't know if you're trying to clap back at me with that or not, but I'm going to take it as a compliment. Everyone does know my prowess."

"Please don't say *prowess* again," Liam said, shaking his head.

"Seriously. Never again." Ethan shivered.

"Hey. All I'm saying is that in the last book I read, prowess is a big thing."

"Stop saying prowess," Lincoln grumbled.

"And for someone who reads the number of romance books that you do, you seriously don't understand women," Ethan said.

"And you do?" Lincoln asked his lover.

Ethan grinned. "Holland thinks so."

"Okay," Lincoln said, a sarcastic note to his tone.

"I don't like your tone, mister."

"You can deal with it later," Lincoln practically purred. Marcus closed his eyes, holding back a laugh.

There had been threats, sure, but they were good-natured. No one was digging, as if they'd always known this was inevitable. Were he and Bristol inevitable? He'd like to think so. Only, sometimes, he wasn't sure. Mostly because he hadn't let himself think about it.

He wasn't going to mess this up, though. He couldn't. Not only because of the people in this room, and what they would do if he did. No, he wouldn't mess this up because he wanted Bristol. There, he'd said it. He wanted her. He wanted to see who they could be together, and what would happen if they took that next step. When they did.

Because tomorrow they would go on a date, and he would be with her. And while they might be going about this relationship backward, they were still making it work.

And he wouldn't let his insecurities hurt her or make the Montgomerys want to take vengeance out on him.

Because the Montgomerys were family, they were steady. Just like he had always thought he was with Bristol.

And so, he was going to make sure that happened. No matter what.

CHAPTER 9

*W*hat did one wear for your first date with your fiancé, when said fiancé was also your best friend and had been in your life for twenty-four years?

"Not what you're wearing, Bristol Montgomery."

She pulled off her top and stood there in black pants and her bra, wondering when she had lost her mind. Oh, probably around ten years ago when she asked her friend and confidante to marry her out of the blue.

And the fact that she kept talking to herself meant that she was beyond the point where she could bring back her sanity. Which was fine, artists were allowed to lose their minds. It helped them create. It assisted with their art.

And if she gagged as she thought that, she didn't blame herself.

What to wear, what to wear.

She pulled off her pants, leaving her in a lacy bra and matching panties. They were new, and totally fuck-me-against-a-door underwear, and she had no idea if they were going to be used tonight.

Was she going to sleep with Marcus? She didn't know. The thought sent shivers through her body, and her stomach clenched. Not to mention her pussy that went wet at the thought.

Well then, apparently, since dream Marcus was very good with his hands, his mouth, and that meaty cock of his, perhaps she hoped real Marcus was the same way.

She really had to stop thinking the phrase *meaty cock* because that sounded weird for anyone other than dream Marcus.

She would not say that to his face, though.

She knew the moment she least expected it, the phrase *meaty cock* would come out, and she would die of mortification.

"Enough of that," she told herself.

She just happened to be wearing pretty panties and a gorgeous bra. Because she liked to wear them. And because she didn't know what was going to happen tonight, so she might as well feel pretty under whatever clothes she decided on.

Had she groomed herself? Yes. Had she shaved her legs? Yes. Had she made sure her hair was smooth and in waves? Yes. She hadn't finished her makeup yet, mostly because she wanted to make sure that it matched her clothes, but at this point, she didn't know. So, she quickly ran to the bathroom to finish up the last of her eyeshadow.

She had everything else done but was seriously worried that she would end up only wearing the pale lavender lace panties and bra.

Her boobs did look great, and as she turned, her ass looked great, too.

Was Marcus going to see that? Who knew?

Because this was just a first date. She generally didn't sleep with anyone on the first date. In fact, she didn't think she ever had.

She frowned, thinking. Nope, never. But this was Marcus. This was different.

And she had done her best to never think about her best friend in this situation, but now she was going to have to because...here they were. She added a bit of color to her eyelids and tried to take deep breaths. Was she going to sleep with Marcus tonight? She didn't know. She didn't know how this date was going to go at all.

She wanted him. She truly wanted him. And that scared her. She hadn't allowed herself to feel the depths of this emotion before. And now that it was an option? She wasn't sure she could actually focus.

But that was Marcus with her. He always made her breath catch, even if she hadn't realized that was what was happening.

The idea of being with Marcus tonight? She had to get the thought out of her head that they were best friends with all their history. She had to go at this like a real date. Because she liked dates. She liked dating.

She liked touching, feeling, laughing. She liked that butterfly sensation within her belly as she tried to suck in a breath and...be.

She wasn't the best at dating, not that great at relationships either. But she tried. Her work took her out of the country often, and sometimes, she had to throw herself into practice, too. Well, that was most of the time.

She did her best to be there for the person she was with, but sometimes, she had to focus on herself. It had taken a lot of therapy, and even more family time for her to realize that that was okay. Marcus had always understood. And the fact that she was somehow getting a chance with him after all this time? It had to mean something. Right?

She let out a deep breath and finished her makeup before going back to her closet. She had a lot of clothes. A lot of shoes, and a lot of bags. Most of it was for work.

She had to meet with dignitaries, and royals, and people who needed to see her in an elevated state, even if most of the time, she wanted to throw her hair on the top of her head and call it a day.

Because of her shows, and thanks to Zia, she had learned to do her hair and her makeup and wore the uniform and costume that a world-renowned cellist would.

But she didn't always feel like that.

Tonight, they were going to their favorite Thai place, something that wasn't too fancy, but it also wasn't run of the mill and fast food.

They had pretty little white bowls and music playing over the speakers. There was never elevator music or pop, but soft, lyrical numbers.

The place had waiters with crisp uniforms and white tablecloths.

It was a place she and Marcus went to for celebrations, and sometimes, if they were having a bad day.

They always took turns paying, even though she was well aware that she made more money than he did.

They never let it be a thing between them, but now that they were getting married? They would have to talk about that.

And about where they would live, and how many children they wanted.

Her heart raced, and she bent down, hands on her knees. Okay, not the time to panic.

Yes, there was a ring on her finger. She looked down at the antique setting and solid heart. But that was merely the beginning. They hadn't talked about the basics, the actual logistics of it all. But that was what tonight was for. A start.

The promise made, the promise kept, and the ring that encircled her finger was only the beginning. Tonight was a chance to follow the road to temptation and peer into a future that neither of them could have imagined.

Because it was all good and well to say that they were engaged and getting married and using those words that still made her breath come in pants, but they needed to truly dive into their feelings and make sure that they were whole when they came out of this. And work on what they meant to each other. And, frankly, what was physically going to happen between the two of them.

Bristol quickly pulled on one of her dresses, a cute red number with a flower pattern on it that had a deep neckline that showed a lot of cleavage. Well, not too much, but enough that it made her feel sexy and happy. It flared out at the hips, and almost resembled a wrap dress.

She liked it because it could be casual or a little fancier, depending on what shoes and jewelry she wore.

She was going for a middle-of-the-road look, so she added a little sparkle on her ears, and then a single rectangular pendant necklace that drew the gaze to her neck—and her boobs.

She couldn't help it, she wanted to look good for Marcus.

Her fiancé. Her friend.

And the man that made her nervous. A feeling she had never felt before. At least, not with him.

That had to count for something. She knew it did.

She took another deep breath and reached for her phone to check what time it was when the doorbell rang.

She froze, her hands shaking. She let out the breath she hadn't realized she'd been holding.

That had to be him.

This was it. The moment. Another moment when everything could change.

She should be used to it by now. But it was hard to think that she could be.

The door opened, and her tongue stuck to the roof of her mouth.

Marcus stood there in black pants, leather shoes, and a black button-up shirt tucked in. He'd rolled up his sleeves to his elbows, showcasing his very delicious forearms. She'd had that thought once before with him, the sight of his forearms doing something very dirty to her. She couldn't help it, they were all muscled with a vein on each that stood out whenever he worked at anything.

They were sexy as hell, and she hadn't realized she had a fetish for forearms until now.

That was good to know, wasn't it?

"You look amazing," Marcus said, his voice husky, low. Dangerous.

She licked her lips, aware she did it far too often in front of him. But the action drew his gaze straight to her mouth, so maybe it was a good thing she did that.

"I was just thinking the same thing about your forearms." She closed her eyes and groaned. "I meant you. But your forearms, too."

She opened her eyes and noticed he had fisted his hands, his forearms looking even more delicious.

Dear God, was she going to faint?

"My forearms?" he asked, laughter in his tone along with something darker, edgier.

"I know. I didn't realize I had a fetish. But here we are."

He threw back his head and laughed, and she relaxed immediately. This was her Marcus. She could be totally honest with him even if she was lying to herself. Because she couldn't lie to him if she didn't know the actual answers. Hence, honesty.

"I called ahead to the Thai place and put our names down on the list in case they were busy. The guy was so excited we were coming in. We're going to have our table."

"Do we go there too often for a place that doesn't have reservations to know us by name?" she asked, grabbing her purse. Marcus reached around and closed the door behind her, making sure it was locked. It was something they did all the time, both acting as if they were so comfortable within each other's homes. They didn't even have to ask each other to keep each other safe.

There was a sense of peace in that. Comfort. Even if it had all been upended by a single promise.

"I think I want that damn soup, so the fact that we won't have to wait for a table? Sounds pretty damn good to me."

Marcus reached out and slid his fingers between hers, and she squeezed his hand, feeling like she was home again. This was normal. Everyday. After all, they went out to lunch and dinner enough to this place to have familiarity.

That was why she was so glad that they were spending their first date like this, rather than trying something new. Everything else was already off-kilter, she needed something steady.

And it sure as hell wasn't going to be her.

"What are you getting?" Marcus asked as he helped her into the car. He closed the door behind her and jogged around the front. She shook her head.

He always did that for her, even before the engagement. See? There was nothing awkward about this. She didn't have to feel nervous.

He sat down next to her, and she inhaled his scent, her nipples going hard.

Okay, apparently, things were different.

"I don't know, probably a stir-fry of some sort. Although I want their spring rolls. Or just everything. I'm starving." She paused. "I sort of didn't eat today."

Marcus started the car and glared at her.

"Why aren't you taking care of yourself?"

"I was working, and I was nervous, okay? Stop."

"No, I'm not. Because you need to take better care of yourself. You skip meals, and then you feel weak, and then you get crabby."

"You're the crabby one," she said and closed her eyes. "Sorry. This is a date. I probably shouldn't be so rude."

"Then you wouldn't be yourself," he quipped, and she glared at him, only to notice that there was laughter dancing in his eyes. She flipped him off, and he laughed.

"See? Now you're flipping me off. It totally feels like a date."

"Are we being awkward about this? And not good at it?"

He reached over and slid his hand across her knee. When he gave it a squeeze, she sucked in a breath, her panties going damp, and her mouth drying.

"Oh, okay, I guess we're doing this. Okay."

They were at a stoplight, so he looked over at where his hand was on her skin, her dress riding up a bit. Shivers ran up her thighs and through the rest of her body, and she almost wanted to squeeze her legs together, trapping his hand. Asking him to go a little bit higher.

Dear God, she was a hussy.

"We're fine, Bristol. Stop overthinking this."

"I wouldn't be me if I weren't overthinking."

"That's the truth." She glared at him again, and he rubbed her knee before turning back to the road and removing his palm. She did not want to feel bereft at the loss, so she ignored it.

But when he reached out and gripped her hand, tangling his fingers with hers, her engagement ring shining in the glow of the streetlights, she let out a relieved breath.

The two of them had always touched, had always held hands, but in the most platonic of ways.

There was nothing platonic now.

Oh, she knew their promise was only an excuse. At least, for her. She had no idea what he was thinking, and she was going to figure it out. But first? She was going to let herself fall.

At least, a little bit.

And hope to hell it wasn't awkward in the end.

By the time they sat at their favorite table, the owner

coming out to see how they were, she was a bundle of nerves and practically squirming in her seat.

She had always thought Marcus attractive, but it was as if there had been a barrier between them before so she didn't have to feel like this.

Now, she couldn't help but pant and want more.

She had truly lost her mind when it came to him, and she couldn't help it. Every touch, every breath, every caress, simply his presence almost sent her over the edge.

And this was only their first date.

"Are my eyes misleading me, or is that an engagement ring?" the owner asked, looking down at Bristol's hand.

She froze for a moment before looking into Marcus's eyes. She could have sworn she saw worry there, and then he smiled, a brilliant one that went straight to her core.

She loved his smile.

"We've been a little busy since we were last here," Marcus said smoothly.

She was grateful that he'd spoken because there was nothing smooth about her right now.

"Finally? Oh, yes. I've always known the two of you were perfect. Huh, always pretending to be only friends. I knew there had to be something more. Dinner's on me tonight."

"Oh, no, don't. Please. Thank you, but you don't have to do that," Bristol said quickly.

"No, no. Dinner's on me." He turned. "My favorite customers are finally engaged. Soon, there will be babies and happiness, and even more family members wanting my food."

Bristol knew she was blushing from head to toe, and Marcus lowered his head, his shoulders shaking.

Was he laughing at the fact that everybody was staring and clapping? Or at the fact that she was bright red like a tomato?

She didn't know, but she had a feeling she would make him pay for this later.

The owner left after the chef brought out an order of spring rolls, tara wings, and nam sod.

Marcus ordered his spicy Tom Yum Goong, while she ordered a Tom Kha Gai for their starters. Then they'd decided to splurge and share Choo Chee Salmon and basil chicken, each of them deciding not to go with curry for the night because they were already too full from the appetizers. However, the leftovers from this place were amazing, and her stomach couldn't help but growl.

She was moaning in ecstasy over her soup, and Marcus looked at her with amusement, shaking his head.

"What?"

"You constantly surprise me with your love for food."

She set down her spoon and tilted her head. "What do you mean?"

"I mean, you always go full-tilt at it. Even though I did just growl at you for not eating enough for the day."

"I am more than making up for it." She patted her belly. "I'm already full over the appetizers and soup, but you know I'm going to eat like half of my dinner."

"And some of mine. I would probably eat the whole thing, but I know how much you love leftovers."

She narrowed her eyes. "You like leftovers as much as I do."

"That's true. And we usually end up watching movies and gorging ourselves on whatever leftovers we can and then order in even more through takeout."

"Wow, don't we sound like gluttons?"

"We don't do it often."

"Often enough."

They grinned at each other and continued eating, laughing at silly things while filling up on tasty and amazing food.

"This is nice," she said suddenly, hoping she was saying the right thing.

Marcus looked at her, tilting his head. "Why, did you think it wouldn't be?"

"I thought it would be awkward and weird."

"We're always awkward and weird. That's us."

"But I don't want things to change." She closed her eyes. "That was stupid." She opened her eyes again. "I don't want *us* to change. Or at least alter the fabric of where we started."

"Then let's not have that happen."

"Okay." He reached out and gripped her hand, then ran his thumb over hers. "Let's start with twenty questions. Or a few questions," he amended.

"What do you mean?"

"Off the top of your head, what are important things to know for someone going into a marriage. Let's start with that. Because we already know everything else about each other. We know our favorite colors, we know how we sleep, we know what our first cars were, our first crushes. We know our first boyfriends and girlfriends. We know all of that. Because we've lived it together. So, let's go into what we want. What do we see our path becoming?"

"That's a really good idea. I feel like I should be taking notes."

He squeezed her hand, and she let out a little sigh. She loved when he did that. "We don't need a notebook. Although, I'm sure you're going to want to write it down later."

"You do know me."

"Okay, so, our future. You and me. What do you want to know?"

"Are you okay if I don't take your last name?" She

asked the first thing that came to her mind. She had no idea why that was it, but there it was.

Marcus nodded. "Professionally, you are Bristol Montgomery. And I know you and your family love your name like a clan. You're even tattooed with it."

"With the Montgomery iris, not the name itself. You were there when I got it."

"I remember. On your hip. Right below where your panties usually lay." His eyes darkened, and she swallowed hard.

"You know, once we're married, you should get it, too. Everyone that moves into the family gets it."

"Like a cult."

"It's not a cult."

"Well, I think you need to call your dad because you're in a cult."

"You listened to like three episodes of that podcast, and you make more jokes about it than I do."

He shrugged.

"Pretty much. Okay, so I don't need you to take my name. Unless you want to legally, instead of professionally. Or, you could even hyphenate it. Whatever you want to do. Because it's not like ownership. You're still going to be the same you, and I'm going to be the same me, and then we're going to figure out what we are together."

"Right. I know that I can't change it for work. It

would be like a pen name at that point if I were an author like Liam."

"That's true."

"And Arden and Holland and even Lincoln are all changing their names. I don't know."

"I know one of your cousin's husbands changed his name to Montgomery for his wife, but I'm not going to do that," Marcus said, laughing.

"Because your mother would hurt me if I tried to get you to do that. No, maybe I'll hyphenate it."

"Maybe I will, too," Marcus said, and she grinned.

"Really?"

"If we have kids, what name would you want them to have? If they have the hyphen, it might be easier if I do, too."

She froze, blinking. "I don't know. I think that's something we'll have to decide when the time comes."

A pause.

"You've always wanted kids, Bristol."

"You have, too."

She swallowed hard, and she noticed that he did, as well.

"So, kids are on the table?" he asked, his voice low.

"Yes. Kids are on the table."

And from there, they went through their lists as if they weren't making such large decisions and talking about important topics that would send any other relationship off-kilter.

But with Marcus? It was everything. She could breathe because she knew he was thinking about it, too.

Because they weren't going back. They were going forward, together.

Somehow.

CHAPTER 10

*M*arcus slid his hand over his face and hoped to hell and back he could figure out what exactly he was going to do next. The date with Bristol? Pretty fucking amazing. Life-affirming even. Things just made sense between them.

He knew that his artistic, brilliant, beautiful friend—*fiancée,* he corrected himself—needed to have complete lists before she could focus on what was important. The idea that the two of them could decide where their thoughts and needs and desires fit in with each other in the long-term meant everything.

They had talked about the essential things, and he knew it was good for her to hear it. Him as well, if he were honest. However, now that they were back at her place, at least in her driveway, things were back to being off. She was sitting in his passenger seat, not looking at him.

Not speaking a word.

Nor was he talking.

Well, hell.

The way they sat in silence probably wasn't the best way to finish the evening. If the evening ended soon at all. Did she want him to come in like before? Only he knew if he went inside, it wasn't going to end like it had when they were merely friends. And if he went home? Fuck. He didn't know.

"I don't know if I should let you in for a drink? Or pretend it's only for coffee? Or let you walk me to the door, and then I'll go and settle in." Bristol was rambling, making her sentences sound like questions rather than pure thoughts, and he was glad for it. Because he knew he would ramble, too.

"I don't think we're finished talking yet," he said, drawing out his words.

"Talking is good. Talking is really good."

Marcus leaned over, undid her seat belt, the back of his hand sliding along her thigh. The sound of her indrawn breath went straight to his cock, and he swallowed hard, his gaze on hers.

"Nothing needs to happen tonight," he whispered.

"But what if it does?" she asked, her voice barely above a whisper.

Bristol licked her lips. Whenever she did, his gaze always went to her mouth, and he couldn't help but want to touch her. Taste her.

"Let's get inside."

"I...okay."

They got out of the car with him waiting at the front, holding out his hand. She slid her palm into his without speaking, and they made their way to her front door. He had a key, but he let her use hers because this wasn't a time where he felt comfortable going in on his own.

They had changed the dynamic of who they were together, as well as who they were apart, and he didn't want to pressure her.

At the same time, he was done ignoring the thoughts and desires he'd had for so long. He couldn't lie to himself anymore and say that he didn't want Bristol. Because he did. He loved the way she tasted, the way she felt. And he wanted his mouth on hers. He wanted to lick across her skin and taste every inch of her. He wanted to see her under him as she writhed. He wanted his hands on her, in her, over her.

He wanted to show her exactly who he was. Not just his body but also his soul. Wanted to do the same with her. He wanted to *know* her.

Part of his mind also wanted to fuck her hard, make her come on his cock, slam her into the wall as they both shook and fell into oblivion. He wanted to do like that old Eric Church song and break the drywall right from the studs.

He wanted to do all of that.

He also wanted to go soft and slow and feel every inch of her.

He didn't know which part they'd get to tonight, but he knew that this was the first step. Or maybe the hundredth, he didn't know anymore.

But this was it. There was no going back. Maybe there never was.

Once they were inside the house, neither of them went to the kitchen for coffee.

He had been inside her home countless times, had even helped her decorate the place because she had done the same for him. She hadn't gone all out but had four bedrooms since she needed an office and a practice space. The other she had made into a guest room for any of her friends from her musical world that came to visit.

He had slept there, as well, mostly when he had more than two drinks and didn't want to drive home. Bristol had slept at his house countless times before, too, because they always had each other's backs, no matter what.

Now, he didn't know what would happen, but if he didn't take this next step, didn't make the move, they were going to be stuck here, wondering what if. At the same time, they had labels for each other that might not make sense to the outside world but totally did to them.

Without them, he wouldn't be able to understand who they were together.

So, why not? Why not make the move?

"Tonight, can I kiss you?" he asked, knowing that, like she had told him a thousand times before: *consent was sexy as fuck.*

She smiled, her cheeks turning a delicious pink.

"I want you to kiss me, Marcus."

He took a step forward, his breath quickening as he loomed over her, her eyes wide as she tilted her head back to look up at him.

"And after I kiss you, can I kiss you again? Can I touch you? Can I taste you?" He lowered his head, his lips brushing her ear. "Can I...fuck you?"

He slid his hands around her, cupping her ass and pressing her body into his. She slipped her arms around his waist, her hands digging into his shirt.

"Please. I thought you'd never ask."

And then his hand was on her thigh, pulling up her skirt, the other in her hair, tilting her head back so he could devour her mouth with his.

This wasn't a casual caress. Wasn't a sweet temptation of sin.

No, this was hard, needful, and fuck-all temptation.

They were both breathing heavily, teeth gnashing as their lips pressed against one another as if they couldn't get enough.

He had his hand up her dress and around to her ass, delving through her thong to her lower lips and into her pussy.

She shouted into his mouth, stiffening at the invasion.

He bit at her lip and kissed away the sting.

"Too much?" he asked, sliding his fingers in and out of her, her body suctioning around him even as she grew wetter.

"Never enough, my God. That is more than a kiss."

"I told you I was going to touch you. That I was going to fuck you." He slid his hands out from under her dress and then licked his fingers clean. "That I was going to taste you."

"My God. I didn't know you were so dirty."

"There's a lot of things that you don't know about me, Bristol Montgomery. Are you ready to learn some?"

She looked at him then and nodded, her eyes dark, her pupils dilated. "Always."

And then they were on each other again, scrambling for each other's clothes. He tugged at her dress, pulling it over her head. Her shoes were still on, but he didn't fucking care. She tugged at his shirt, the buttons flying free, and they laughed, all while kissing, licking, touching. She undid his belt, and then he was toeing off his shoes, his pants down around his ankles.

He cursed, then reached down to get a condom out of his pocket. She raised her brows.

"I'm always going to be safe with you, damn it. And you know my dad has been throwing condoms at me since I was like fourteen."

Bristol laughed. "My mom's been doing the same."

"And that's enough mentioning them right now," he said and then sheathed his dick.

Her eyes moved down the length of him, and he squeezed the base of his cock, cupping his balls.

"You know, I've felt the line before. I've sort of seen an outline whenever you wear those very sexy gray pants. I'm pretty sure you're a grower and a show-er."

He grinned, then moved forward. "Yeah?"

"Yeah."

And then his lips were on hers again, his dick pressed between them. She was still wearing her lacy bra and panty set and her heels, looking fucking sexy as hell.

"Keep the heels on," he ordered, and then he shoved her panties to the side and played with her again, using his thumb along her clit as he slowly rubbed her seam. She arched for him, her shoulders pressed against the wall, and she leaned in to his touch.

He fucked her with his hand as he lowered the cups of her bra so he could lick her rosy pink nipples.

They were tight buds on precious skin and begged for his mouth.

So, he licked, he sucked, and he wanted more.

"Are you going to come for me, Bristol?" he asked, his voice low. Bristol shook against him.

"Marcus," she whispered, and then he plunged into her with his fingers, playing with her clit as he did, his mouth on her nipples.

She shattered around him, her pussy clamping around his fingers, but he kept going, and then he fell to his knees, needing to taste her, lap her up.

"Marcus!"

"Shh, baby. Let me take care of you."

And then his mouth was on her, and he was drowning in her taste. She was sweet, like honey, and he needed her. He slid one leg over his shoulder, and her other leg started to shake, so he kept his hand on her thigh, holding her steady. He used his free hand to spread her before he licked and sucked, lashing his tongue over her clit.

"How are you so good at that?"

"All for you, baby," he whispered, and she laughed before she called out his name, her pussy clamping around him again as he sucked off her clit as she came.

And then he was on his feet, his hands on her thighs as he lifted her up and pressed her against the wall.

"Marcus," she whispered.

He looked at her and swallowed hard. "Are you ready?" he asked, suddenly a little worried, a bit shy.

"I've been waiting for you," she whispered, her hands on his face. Then he slid inside her, slowly at first, inch by inch, their gazes never breaking, both of them holding their breath as if they'd been waiting for this moment for longer than either of them cared to admit.

Suddenly, he was fully seated, her body stretching to take him in, her legs shaking as she wrapped her calves around his back. He moved one hand so he could cup her face, wiping tears from under her eyes, knowing he wasn't hurting her, but that this was something different. Something he hadn't expected.

He knew this woman. Knew her from the bottom of his soul all the way to hers. He had known they would always be connected, that no matter what happened in the world, they would be together. And they had made sure that they would always have that path to one another. Even if it hadn't ended up like this. Yet it had brought the two of them here, to this moment in time.

As he filled her, and she cried against him, her hands on him as he struggled not to move, he simply looked at her. And he knew.

No matter what he had told himself, he would have come to this moment.

This would be etched on his soul until the end of his days.

He had been lying to himself when he'd said that it was only a promise to a friend to see what would happen.

He loved Bristol Montgomery. Not as his best friend,

not as the other half of his soul, but as a woman that he knew would be part of him forever.

He loved her, and he had no idea if she loved him the way that he needed her to.

But right then, with the feeling of her around his cock and in his heart, he didn't care.

Because he'd find a way to make that happen.

But first, he had to finish this, needed to complete their connection, and he needed to be with her.

So, he pushed thoughts of what could be out of his mind because he knew he wouldn't be able to focus if he were worried about the future and placed his mouth on hers. And then he moved.

She was still wearing her bra, her panties pushed to the side, and her shoes digging into his back, and he didn't care. It was hot as hell, and this was his Bristol. The love of his life.

The only love of his life.

The sweetest lie he had ever told himself.

They made love—because this wasn't merely fucking anymore, this wasn't just sex, it was what he had always worried he'd feel if he let himself.

She arched into him, her nails raking down his back, and he plunged deeper, needing more.

"Marcus," she whispered.

A kiss. A breath. Another kiss. "My Marcus."

And then he was lost, his mouth on hers as he took in

her scream. Her coming around him as he followed her into ecstasy.

His legs shook, and he slammed into her one more time, both of them arching into each other as if they couldn't get their fill, as if they couldn't get close enough.

And afterward, he helped her to her feet, and he cleaned her up, leading her to her bathroom so they could shower and make sure she was taken care of. Because that's who he was.

The man who always cared for her, not because he had to, but because he wanted to. And because she did the same for him.

And then they were in bed, kissing, touching, this time their lovemaking sweeter, softer, as if they had taken off the edge yet needed more.

They didn't need to speak anymore because they would later, they always had time.

And when she fell asleep in his arms, he held her close and hoped to hell that they wouldn't run away from this.

Because he had spent the entirety of his life telling himself that he and Bristol Montgomery were great as just friends.

But there was nothing just about the two of them.

This was the woman he loved, the woman that he was going to marry, and the woman that he would make sure he deserved.

He only hoped like hell that he'd develop that plan.

Because as she snuggled into him, he knew he didn't want this to end.

Only he was afraid that if he weren't careful, the ending would hit them harder than either of them ever expected.

CHAPTER 11

"*I*t's not supposed to be weird, is it?" Bristol asked as Marcus leaned against the doorjamb.

When he gave her a lazy smile, her insides twisted, and she nearly had to press her thighs together.

What was it about a man leaning against a doorjamb and giving that lazy smile? It was as if they knew what they were doing and just wanted to burst ovaries all around the room—adding to the fact that Marcus had on a button-up shirt that he had rolled to his elbows.

She nearly bit into her knuckle to hold back a moan.

Dear God, she wanted to jump her librarian and strip him down and taste every inch of him.

She'd already done that nearly an hour ago, but she was ready for round three, no matter that not a lot of time had passed.

The fact that her sex drive seemed to have ramped up when it came to Marcus shouldn't have been a surprise. After all, she had been hiding her feelings for him within her mind for years.

Now that she was finally letting herself want him, dear God, she couldn't do anything *but* want him.

Today, however, was filled with things that had nothing to do with wanting to sleep with her best friend and fiancé.

No, today was the Montgomery family dinner.

And she was terrified she was going to fuck it up.

"You're going to be fine. Besides, this is your family. I should be the nervous one."

She pulled her shirt over her head, ignored the groan that slid from Marcus's lips, and tried not to smile. The fact that he liked the way she looked? The fact that he growled at her covering up? That might make her day. Only she was going to do her best not to lean too much into that particular feeling because everything was still so new. She might have that rock on her finger, and they might have made promises to one another, but there was still part of their relationship that was brand new. Infinitesimal and in its infancy. And it gave her butterflies to think about it.

"Wait, aren't you nervous?" she asked, pulling herself out of her thoughts about the man in front of her and putting her attention on him instead.

Marcus shrugged as he leaned away from the door-jamb. "Maybe. I mean, your family's always intimidating."

Her eyes widened, confused. "Not to you. You're practically family yourself."

"Well, let's hope they don't want to adopt me, or that's going to get a little tricky when we're finishing up our marriage license."

Her lips twitched. "You know Mom and Dad never wanted to adopt you. Mostly because your mom and dad would murder mine."

"Don't lie. My folks wouldn't murder your parents. Maybe a little maiming. Though if yours did adopt me, my parents would want to be adopted, as well. You know, one big, happy family."

"Our mothers did seem excited about the engagement."

"Hell, yeah. It's everything the two of them have ever wanted. I like that our families have always been friends."

"Yeah, unlike Lincoln's family." She had no idea why she'd brought her future brother-in-law up, but she and Marcus had discussed Lincoln often since he was part of their family, too.

Marcus shook his head. "Not the whole of his family. Lincoln's parents are nice. They just moved on to a different part of their lives without him. Adults do that. Not everybody lives in the same state for their entire lives. Hell, I'm surprised that you didn't end up moving to New York or L.A. or something."

"I would never do that. I love my parents. My family." She paused. "And I didn't want to be away from you either because you were always part of that. My touchstone."

"Well, I'm glad you came back. And I'm fucking glad that I got a job at a library here. It's not as easy as some might think, even though it's a big city."

"Well, we're not down in Denver, we're up in Boulder. Though if you had gotten a job down in Denver, that wouldn't have been too far for everybody."

"That's true. But I'm glad that I got a job here, and one that's not technically part of the university so I don't have to constantly deal with that type of work politics."

"Your job has enough of it as it is."

"That is true."

"Anyway, we need to get going. You don't want to be the last one at your house."

"No, because then Aaron will lord it over all of us."

"He is the pesky younger brother sometimes, isn't he?" Marcus asked, a smile on his lips. She leaned forward and kissed those lips, unable to hold back. It was so weird. Before, Bristol would hug him or want to kiss his cheek, or maybe hold his hand without thinking too hard on the matter. Now that there was this new layer, this new dynamic between them, she didn't want it to stop. Were they going to kiss each other in public? Well, they sort of had when they'd been on their date, hadn't they? Although public, and then in front of the Montgomerys, were two different things. Entirely.

"Why do you have that look on your face?" Marcus asked, tucking her hair behind her ear. She leaned into his hold like she always did; that part never changed between them. It was the additional components of what they were becoming that were making everything sticky.

"What if things are weird, *weirder* than they already kind of are sometimes?"

"I don't think it's going to be too bad. I've already hung out with the guys, you with the girls, and each of us has seen our parents since we started this new phase."

"I know, but this is the first time it's us in front of the family together. I don't know. I just don't want things to be awkward."

Marcus nodded, frowning even as he traced her cheek with his fingertip. He had done that for ages. It was nothing new. Except now, she focused on how those fingers had felt on her when they were making love, when they were touching...other places. And she didn't quite know how to breathe when it came to that.

Maybe she should. Perhaps she should think logically and make a list. But that wasn't going to happen when it came to him. There was nothing logical about how she felt about Marcus because she had done so well hiding those feelings. She'd pushed down what she should have rather than what she wanted for so long, that she didn't know how to put a title or a price on that nameless emotion that ran through her.

"I don't want to ruin everything," she whispered.

"It's the two of us, Bristol. We can't ruin it."

"I don't know. I'm excellent at fucking things up."

"No, you're not. You excel at everything you do. Including making sure others know that they're not alone. You helped Arden figure out that she could be part of the Montgomerys right away."

Bristol snorted. "No, I invaded her house and told her I was going to be her friend, with or without Liam. I didn't like the fact that she had hidden herself away because she was sick. Not that it was my right to make any of those calls, but I hated that she felt alone. And you know I have space for friends. And Arden seemed like a great person."

"And you're a great person, too. You guys are friends, with or without Liam, like you said. And it's because you're an amazing woman. You reached out, even though it was a little stalkerish."

She groaned, closing her eyes tightly. "Not too stalkerish, right?"

"I'm going to plead the fifth on that one and then move the conversation to Holland. Your other stalker victim."

"I am not a stalker. *You* are."

"That doesn't even make sense."

"Perhaps. Still, I don't know. I didn't want Holland to be alone either. I mean, she ran out on her wedding because her fiancé was a douchebag." She paused. "Thank you for not being a douchebag."

He kissed her again, softly, their tongues tangling. Her knees went weak. "I promise never to be that type of douchebag. I may, you know, be an asshole sometimes. But that can't be helped."

She snorted. "Okay, whatever you say. However, I like Holland, too. And, yes, I did just show up at her house to make sure that she knew who to talk to beyond my brother and Lincoln. And maybe that could be weird to other people. I didn't think so."

"That wasn't too weird. Not in the grand scheme of things. You're friends."

"And, my next project, I mean, *person* I'm going to make sure knows that they are welcome as part of the family is Madison."

Marcus's brows furrowed. "You're not going to play matchmaker, are you? Because Lincoln's cousin doesn't need a match. She could probably do that on her own."

Bristol raised a single brow. "Are you saying that because you think she's hot?"

He grinned, and she nearly growled." Of course, I think she's hot. Now, don't get all weird about that. You and I have talked about the fact that we both think she's hot."

"Perhaps. But now that we're engaged, isn't that weird?"

"I don't know. I always thought it was kind of cool that since we're both bi, we've been able to check out the same people. But I suppose I could refrain from finding anyone attractive from here on out."

"Well, I do kind of like going over our celebrity crushes together. It always made me feel like we were best friends for a reason."

"We're best friends for more reasons than our crush on Michael B. Jordan."

"And Jennifer Garner. We cannot forget the days of *Alias*."

Marcus grinned, shaking his head. "You're right. We can never forget those days. Though I still don't understand the red wig."

"You're not supposed to. All you have to know is that it made her look pretty."

"Whatever you say. Now, we're going to be late, but you have to promise me not to matchmake with Madison."

"Why?"

"Because you don't do matchmaking well. We both know this."

"That was one time, and I didn't realize they were

cousins."

"They had the same last name, and I'm pretty sure you met them both at a family barbecue that they invited the neighbors to."

"I thought one of them had to be a neighbor. I also cannot believe that we're still having this conversation."

"I'm just saying," he whispered.

"Stop. I'm not going to matchmake. I'm going to friend-make." She groaned. "Okay, that doesn't make sense. Madison is slowly coming into my web." She paused again, while Marcus's eyes danced with laughter. "That is not what I meant either."

"Oh, I'm picturing you with this web of friends and acquaintances that you're slowly bringing together, your little legs working as you weave."

"Shush. As I was saying, Madison's family sucks, we all know that. And she's finally hanging out with us a little more. So, I'm going to make sure she knows that she's welcome to be one of us."

"I'm not going to repeat it for you. I don't think you're a cult."

"No, I wasn't expecting you to. And we're not a cult. We're the Montgomerys."

"Your family motto?"

She growled. "Now, really, we need to get going."

He paused before they moved. "Will Madison be there?"

"Yes, because she's coming with Lincoln." She grinned prettily, batting her eyes.

"You talked to Lincoln about it, didn't you?"

"No, I talked to Ethan because he was closer to me, and he talked to Lincoln."

"Oh, the web you weave."

"Ack. Stop," she said, laughing. The drive to her parents' house was relatively quick, and she still marveled at the fact that, somehow, she was able to live near most of her family in an age where not everyone was able to do that.

"I'm so grateful that your family and mine all still live here. I mean, I know Liam and I moved around a bit, mostly because of work, but now we're all here. You know?"

Marcus reached out and pressed her knee again, and even though her stomach clenched, mostly at his nearness, she still relaxed, the familiar touch soothing.

"I get it. I don't know what I would do if I had to live far from my family. I'm spoiled that way."

"The fact that all three of your sisters got married and still moved near you is insane."

"Your family's the same way. Hell, like ninety percent of your cousins even live in the state."

"I think it's about a hundred percent right now. And one recently moved back."

"That's pretty remarkable."

"We're a close family." She paused. "And not a cult."

"So you say. But here I am, about to get sworn in. Do I get a robe or something?"

"No, you get ink seared into your flesh."

Marcus looked at her and then laughed as he parked in front of her parents' house. "You're right, the fact that your family has a tattoo that even those who get married in receive, tells me it's closer to a cult than you think."

"Jerk." She laughed as they got out of the car. Marcus slid his arm around her waist and kissed her firmly on her mouth, even as she laughed against him.

"Still a cult," he whispered.

"There you guys are. I'm so glad you're here." Her mother clapped from the doorway, beaming. Okay, it seemed that they were going with the PDA and acting natural.

Because this was natural, they were genuinely getting married. They were figuring out their future. And they were kissing, touching as if they always had. As if it had always been a part of their lives.

The fact that she was still nervous and trying to contemplate what would happen next wasn't something she would focus on tonight.

"Come in. We're doing appetizers right now."

Bristol frowned. "Are we the last here?" she asked.

Her mother shrugged as she came up to them, giving Bristol a kiss on the cheek, and then going up onto her toes as Marcus leaned down so she could do that to his cheek, as well.

"Yes, but Aaron was early, mostly because I think he wanted to be first to beat you."

"Darn baby brother."

"You know he still thinks of himself as a big brother. I don't know, must be that little-brother complex," her mother said, laughing.

"And yet, I'm the one with the middle-child complex?" Ethan asked as he came out to the front door.

"Come on in. We're eating bruschetta and Caprese salad."

"Oh, that sounds yummy, but I thought we were having roast with potatoes," Bristol said. "I didn't know you served those together."

Her mom smiled. "I was in the mood. However, they didn't have the roast that I wanted at the store, so we're doing roasted chicken stuffed with some lemons and fresh herbs. And of course, mashed potatoes, asparagus, Brussel sprouts, glazed carrots, and then scalloped potatoes on the side."

"I think I may just fall in love with you," Marcus said, smiling widely. "Seriously, I'm starving."

"Then go eat bruschetta." Her mother narrowed her eyes at Bristol. "Why aren't you feeding this man? You know your duty."

Bristol resisted the urge to flip her mother off but did

roll her eyes. "Yes, because I believe you when you say it's my duty to make sure my man is fed."

"You called him your man. I'm so excited about this." She kissed Bristol's cheek again and then tugged Marcus off to the food.

Her dad sidled up at that point, giving Bristol a big hug. "Ignore your mother. She likes poking at you. And you know I'm the one that made the appetizers."

"Is that why they don't match dinner?"

"Your mother was in the mood for a lot of tomatoes, even though it didn't go with the rest of her theme. So, today, it's simply food that we were in the mood for rather than a theme. We're allowed to do that."

"And today was the day that you didn't allow us to bring anything for dinner."

"No, but that's because now that you're all adults, we've switched it up so we have Montgomery dinners at all of your houses, as well, not only ours."

"Liam is next, right?"

"And then Ethan's family, and then you and Marcus. Aaron will bring up the rear."

"As always, the baby, the one that's forgotten."

"Really?" Madison asked from the side, laughing. "You have inserted yourself in every conversation since I got here. I'm pretty sure nothing is *forgotten* with you," she said.

Bristol slapped her hands together. "Madison. You're

here. And you're my new favorite person. We must put Aaron down. That is the one rule of being part of our cult —I mean, our clan."

"Told you it's a cult," Marcus said from the other side of the room, a little plate put together. He had another dish in his hand and held it up towards her. "Hungry?" he asked.

She smiled and went over to him, taking her plate.

"Thank you."

"Always."

"You know, I realized that you guys have always done this, but it's kind of weird seeing it with that ring on your finger."

She looked over at Ethan. "What do you mean?" she asked, suddenly self-conscious. She played with her engagement ring with her thumb, twisting it around her finger.

"I'm not saying anything bad," Ethan said quickly, both of his lovers glaring at him. "I'm not."

"I think what he meant was that we are new to the idea of you and Marcus truly together and out in the open. One day, I'm sure you'll tell us the story of how it all happened, but since you have given us the decency of not diving into every single personal aspect of our relationship, I'll refrain from doing so now with yours." Lincoln smiled as he said it, sounding ever the gentleman, and Bristol sank into Marcus's side, a little relieved.

"I didn't say I would hold back," Aaron added, and let out an *oof* when Madison elbowed him in the gut.

"Stop it," she whispered.

"You don't even know me, and now you're injuring me? Lincoln, take your cousin."

"Madison, I permit you to do whatever you need to Aaron. Beat him up. He probably deserves it."

Madison smiled at her cousin. "Thank you. You know I do feel like I'm part of the family now."

"Yeah, me, too," Aaron grumbled, and Bristol laughed, watching the others as they joked around.

Liam and Arden came from the back room, looking a little tousled, and everyone did their best not to start laughing.

"Sorry, we were just taking Jasper out."

The white Siberian Husky took that moment to walk up to all of them, needing pets. He didn't beg for food, he was a very well-behaved dog, but she knew that at least Aaron was going to feed him some scraps.

Bristol wouldn't, mostly because she knew that the others would, and they didn't want to overwhelm him. But she loved that dog. And if she were home enough, she'd get one of her own. But it wasn't fair.

Maybe she would get one now that Marcus would be home. And then she frowned, guilt and tension turning in her gut. What would happen when she went on tour? Would he go with her? No, he couldn't. He had a full-time job, one he loved. But how would they do apart?

And what would happen once they were married and had children? Would she stay home? Would he? She didn't know the answer, and they were going to have to talk it out. But they were still in the beginning phases, and it didn't matter what label they put on themselves, she didn't know if they were ready.

Marcus squeezed her shoulder and looked down at her.

"What's wrong?"

She did her best to clear her face and shook her head. "Nothing. Overthinking."

"You know you're not supposed to do that."

"I know. I can't help it. Now, I'm going to eat some bruschetta, and then I'm going to pick on my baby brother. Because I can."

"I have a feeling Madison's doing that for you."

"I knew she was my favorite," she said quickly, pushing all thoughts of what could potentially be a disaster from her mind. Because she was so afraid of what might happen when they looked beneath the surface of this new part of themselves and realized that it didn't work.

What if it didn't? And what if, with a single kiss, and a single promise, they had ruined everything they'd had forever?

CHAPTER 12

*N*ow Marcus understood precisely what Bristol had been feeling a week prior when she had once again introduced him to the family.

Not quite an introduction since he literally had a stocking at their house for Christmas. But it had been the first time he had gone with Bristol as her fiancé. Though he hadn't had to deal with the interrogations, he still felt as if the questions might have come at any moment if he hadn't been aware. In fact, everybody had been extraordinarily cautious about how they treated his relationship with Bristol.

The whole event made him feel like the Montgomerys might have an inkling that things weren't quite standard when it came to them.

He had somehow survived that whole ordeal

unscathed because he had a feeling everybody was waiting to see what would happen between the two of them.

Maybe they were walking on eggshells as he and Bristol were.

Tonight, however, wasn't about them. No, it was about *his* family.

He had no idea how bringing Bristol to dinner was going to work out, but he had to go into it with high hopes.

Not that he was too worried about the idea that his family would treat her poorly. They never had in the past. His parents loved her like she was already their daughter. Bristol had always gotten along with his sisters as if she had been part of their family from the beginning.

His siblings had bugged him relentlessly about his connection to Bristol over the years. They'd always wanted to know how the relationship had evolved over time, though Marcus couldn't explain it himself. His sisters had never been cruel or rude towards Bristol. Just like the Montgomerys had never been so towards him. Aaron might have been an ass a little bit a couple of weeks before while they were figuring out exactly how the relationship had started, but Marcus didn't blame him. Oh, he was still going to keep the details to himself, but he didn't blame Aaron for wanting to know. Marcus himself had grilled his sisters' husbands. Mostly for show because he liked the guys. He hoped this would be the same thing. The other Montgomerys had shielded him from that, and he was grateful.

Tonight, however, was all about the Stearn family.

"I'm going to throw up."

Marcus looked over at Bristol as she fisted her hands on her knees in the passenger seat of his car. She had on gray slacks and a sweater cape thing that made him think of a flying squirrel. He had told her that once before, and she had glared at him and stalked out of the room. That had been a year ago, and she still wore the damn thing, so she must like it. He loved the way it looked on her, but he always thought about the squirrel.

"Why are you going to throw up?"

"First, I know that look. You're thinking about the squirrel and my shirt. And that's just rude. I look amazing in this top. It gives me an hourglass figure even while it's a cape. Like it makes no sense, and yet I love it. And your sisters love this shirt. So, I figured I would wear it for good luck. Don't talk about the squirrel."

He snorted, shaking his head. "How the hell could you know what I was thinking about without even truly looking at me?" he asked, and she shrugged.

"You're my best friend. I know things like that. Plus, you get that little smirk when you're trying not to laugh at something you know annoys me. And since the only thing in this car that I know of that annoys you is my shirt, fuck you very much."

"So, if I was thinking about something else that makes me laugh, you'd try to hit me?"

"No, mostly because you're driving, and I want to make it to your parents' home safe." She paused, her lips quirking into a smile. "Thank you for trying to get my mind off the fact that I'm going to throw up."

Marcus frowned. "You said you thought you were going to throw up. Are you actually going to throw up now?" he said, looking for a place to pull over.

"I'm not truly going to throw up. At least, I don't think so." She put her hand on her stomach over the squirrel top.

His lips quirked again.

"Stop fucking thinking about squirrels."

He burst out laughing, and she joined him, both of them shaking their heads as he took the next turn.

"I'm just nervous. This is your family. Your parents. Your sisters and their men. It's scary."

"You've been over to my house as many times as I've been to yours."

"It doesn't always feel like that. Maybe that's because I'm self-centered."

"Shut up."

"You shut up."

They laughed again, the tension easing.

"I just don't want to make a bad impression."

"They know you. You've slept over at my parents' house when I wasn't even there."

He could tell she'd narrowed her eyes at him even if he wasn't looking. She always did with this particular story. "We were in middle school, and I was supposed to do my astronomy project with you and stay the night. Only you forgot and decided to have a slumber party at your friend's house. You know, with the boys. Instead of inviting any of the girls."

"Boy-girl slumber parties weren't a good thing back then."

"It was never a problem with us before. But I showed up, my sleeping bag under my arm, and my tiny little telescope ready to go. And your mom took one look at me and promptly cursed your name."

"That sounds like my mother," he said, rolling his eyes as he took the next turn.

"Well then, your mom had me come inside, and your parents, along with your sisters, played with me in the back yard and helped me with my astronomy lesson. My parents were all ready to come and pick me up and apologize for the confusion. Mostly because my dad had talked to your dad, but our moms hadn't really talked to one another about the plan."

Marcus snorted. "And that meant that the dads got in

trouble, too. After all, they aren't supposed to plan things without putting it all on the calendar."

"You know it," she said, smiling. "But it was one of the best times. Your dad knew all about astronomy, and we had this program on your old computer that helped us figure out the constellations that we couldn't determine from the book. It was a blast. I wish you would've been there."

"I was going over to the guy's house to go talk about girls. You know, about how gross they were."

"You were in middle school. Were girls really gross then?"

Marcus shrugged. "Maybe not. But *we* were pretty gross."

"That is true."

They pulled into his parents' neighborhood, and he parked right in front of the house, turning off the engine but not getting out yet. He undid his seatbelt and turned a little so he could look directly at Bristol. "Everything's going to be fine. You and me? We're getting this done."

"Getting this done?" she asked, her eyebrows raised.

Marcus winced.

"I mean, they love you. We're going to go in there, we're going to have some dinner, and they're most likely going to grill me. Not you."

Bristol snorted. "You are the baby. The perfect one. They're not going to grill you."

"You act as if you've never met my family."

"Didn't we recently go over the fact that I do know them?" she asked him, leaning forward.

Because he couldn't help himself, and he kind of liked this new part of their relationship, he leaned forward and laid the gentlest of kisses on her lips. "Let's go inside. They're not going to wait for long."

The tap on this window scared the crap out of both of them, and Bristol yelped, while Marcus laughed.

"Apparently, we don't have to wait long at all."

"Here they are."

He turned to see Vanessa standing outside the car, tapping the glass. She had a wide grin on her face, even as she shook her head.

He and Bristol got out, and Jennifer and Andie on the other side of their car hugged Bristol close.

But he didn't have anything to worry about. Right? His family loved her. Just because he was a little nervous about what they would think about how quickly everything was happening, didn't mean that they would treat Bristol wrong.

They might grill him, but he probably deserved that. After all, this was out of left field.

But in the end, he didn't want to hurt his family, especially his mother, by going back on the promises they had made.

"Look at you, making out with your fiancée instead of

coming inside." His sister kissed him on the cheek and then smacked him on the arm.

"Did you bring what you were asked to?"

Marcus nodded and then went to the back seat of his car to get out the two bottles of wine and the cookies.

"Bristol and I made them ourselves."

"You guys bake together?" Andie asked, clasping her hands in front of her. "How cute."

"Are they edible?" Jennifer asked and ducked out of the way of Andie, trying to elbow her in the gut.

"Hey. I'm not making fun of you. I'm making fun of our baby brother. That's always been allowed. Now that he actually has a woman that we all like and love doesn't mean I can't make fun of him still."

"They are totally edible," Bristol said, laughing. "And thank you for thinking that if they weren't edible, it would be his fault instead of mine. Because we all know that he's the one that knows how to cook and bake. I literally burned a pan trying to boil water once."

"You were practicing and forgot to turn off the burner. It happens."

"And you constantly read and listen to books while you cook, and you don't boil shit over."

"Look at you guys, fighting but not really fighting." Andie danced from foot to foot. "You are so cute. Now, come on in because you know Mom and Dad are watching us from inside."

Marcus looked over at the house, and indeed, his parents were waving from the window.

"Oh right, it's damp out here. I bet your dad doesn't want your mom out, just in case."

Everybody looked at each other and smiled softly while Bristol winced. "I'm sorry." He reached out and rubbed her lower back.

"No, we bring it up often. We worry about her to the point that we annoy her. That's what makes us family. So, make sure you annoy her, too. Because you cannot be the favorite among us."

"I thought Chris was the favorite," Marcus said dryly, speaking of Andie's husband.

"He is." Andie sighed.

Jennifer rolled her eyes. "The husbands are in the house, mostly because we asked them not to come out so we could bug you."

Vanessa added, "It took all of their willpower, and our clear restraint to make it happen. So, we need to go in. Let the grilling commence."

"Be nice to Bristol," Marcus said.

"Bristol's safe. We love her, and we're excited to see her part of the family. You on the other hand... You're the one that we're going to grill."

With more ribbing, they made their way into the house, where his mother was already hugging Bristol tightly as his father took her bag and hung it on the hook by the door.

"You're here," his mother said and kissed him on the cheek. He wrapped his arms around her and hugged her tight, inhaling the scent that reminded him of home and the woman who had always been with him no matter what.

When he had almost lost her, he'd thought he had nearly lost a piece of himself. Maybe he had lost part of himself along the way anyway.

But having her there, having her so fucking happy? He was finding his way back.

And as he looked over his mother's head at Bristol, he figured that maybe he was finding more of his way with her.

It should scare him, but it didn't. Bristol had always been there. Now that he was allowing himself to think about who she could be with him beyond what they always had, everything that he had hidden for so long was now bubbling up to the surface, ready to erupt.

It had only taken an accidental misunderstanding and a promise that some people would never comprehend for it to happen.

They ate, drank, and laughed. Nobody grilled him, or her. Didn't make any sense to him. They should be interrogating them. They should be wondering how the hell they had decided to become engaged out of the blue, but nobody was asking. Maybe they were too afraid that if they did, the bubble would burst, and everything would go back to the way it was. But it couldn't go back to the way it was. Marcus wasn't sure he would let it.

"So, that wasn't as bad as I thought it would be," Bristol said, taking out her hair clip and rubbing her scalp.

Marcus set down the empty Tupperware, not that the cookies were all eaten, and took out his wallet and keys, toeing off his shoes. It felt as if they were coming home after a long day, where they lived together, and this was their future. It was a glimpse of it. They hadn't nailed down where they would live or when their wedding would be, but they would get there. He figured they would do this dating thing for a while and just be. And then the rest would come. Because if he stressed himself out too much, trying to figure out exactly what was going to happen, it wouldn't work out.

"I don't think it went bad at all. For you."

"Simply because your sisters cornered you while their husbands laughed didn't mean it went badly."

"See, I don't know how I ended up on the outside of this because my sisters are on your side. They love you. Because you're a woman. And then my brothers-in-law are on your side because you're going to be part of the family. How did I end up on the outside of both versions?"

Bristol laughed and put her hands on his chest. "You

know you're not on the outside. Not with my family, and not with yours. And the fact that they were giving us space to figure this out is a little shocking and quite worrying."

Her words echoed his thoughts, and he nodded and tucked her hair behind her ears. "Yeah, I think they all know something's different. But they're letting us figure it out on our own."

"Which doesn't always happen with our families."

Marcus snorted. "Yeah, not even a little. That should worry me, but I don't want to focus on it too much. You know?"

Bristol nodded and then went up on her tiptoes to kiss his jaw.

He grinned and slowly slid his hands down her sides to grip her butt. She smiled.

"Well, hello there, Mr. Marcus."

"You're right. This squirrel shirt does give you curves."

She punched him in the chest.

"How dare you?"

Marcus snorted. "If that little fist of yours had done any damage, maybe I'd be a little offended."

"My hands are insured, mister. These babies are my livelihood. I'm not going to hurt them by punching you."

"At least, you didn't tuck your thumb in."

"Of course, I didn't. My brothers trained me. And those self-defense classes I took."

"I forgot you took those," Marcus said, his voice lowering.

"Liam made me take them before my first tour. Remember? Before my birthday."

Marcus let out a breath. "I remember. The birthday that seemed to change everything."

"Yeah, but for the better, right?" she asked, her voice low.

Marcus didn't know what to say, because he thought so, but what if he was wrong? What if this was only the beginning of the end?

He let that dreadful thought slide through him, and instead of answering, he pressed his mouth to hers and moaned.

He kissed her, putting everything into it, putting himself into it.

There would be a time soon that kisses and touches wouldn't be enough. They would have to face what their future held.

But for now, this wasn't it.

For now, they would breathe, and they would just be.

The future could come in the morning. And they would face it.

He hoped to hell it would be together, though.

CHAPTER 13

"*I* thought you had the day off?" Ronin asked as he walked into Marcus's office. Marcus lifted his head and pulled off his reading glasses. He didn't need them all the time, but when he spent his working hours looking at minuscule text, his eyes strained a bit. Plus, they had blue light blockers for his computer. The fact that Bristol seemed to like them on him was a plus.

He held back a smile, thinking about her. She'd always been on his mind, only in a far different way than she was now. The idea that he was allowed to think of her this way? To want more? It should worry him. But it didn't.

He fucking loved it.

"What?" Marcus asked, pulling his thoughts away

from Bristol and precisely what they meant to one another.

Ronin snorted. "I asked why you were here since I thought you were off today. And look at you, diving into work, getting distracted, and from the look on your face at that last moment, you weren't thinking about work at all. Bristol?"

Marcus pinched the bridge of his nose, mostly because he hated wearing glasses for too long, and pushed away from his desk, stretching his back.

"I've been focusing on work today, but I was only going to take the afternoon off, not the whole day."

"That doesn't put you over hours?" Ronin asked, coming to sit across the desk.

"We're always over hours," Marcus said with a laugh. "That's why we don't get paid by the hour."

"Touché."

"But anyway, I was in the middle of this one part yesterday, and I wanted to come in and finish it. But I'm heading down to Denver in a little bit, so don't worry, I won't bother you for long."

"That's not why I'm here, and you know it. You're not bothering me at all, dork."

"Hey, we're at work, don't call me a dork."

Ronin just smiled. "Maybe. I'm on break, and you're heading out soon, so...two seconds?"

"Okay," Marcus said a little cautiously.

"When's the wedding?" Ronin inquired, and Marcus snorted.

"Aaron?" Marcus asked, and Ronin shrugged. "Yeah, he came in for a couple of texts we have that he can't get online and was talking to me about it. Why didn't you tell me you and Bristol were engaged?"

"I think it's mostly because it doesn't feel real," Marcus said honestly, the words falling from him before he even thought to dial it back.

"Is there something wrong?" Ronin asked, a little cautious. "Do you want to tell me exactly what's going on?"

Marcus shook his head. "No, that's between Bristol and me. Is that okay?"

Ronin tilted his head and frowned. "You know part of my past. Right?"

Marcus nodded, knowing that it wasn't a secret, but not something that Ronin talked about often. After all, Ronin hadn't always been a librarian. The other man had seen things that nobody should see. Had gone through shit that had taken so much from him. But now Ronin was here and looked happy. For all that Marcus could tell.

"So, you know part of what I went through, and because of that, you know that sometimes you have to face what's right in front of you and lean on those near you to get through."

"Yeah, I know," Marcus said softly.

"I think Bristol is perfect for you. She makes you smile every time you talk about her. She's hilarious, talented, and of course, hot as fuck."

Marcus was happy that Ronin had shut the door earlier because this wasn't the best place to talk about things like this.

"You know the pearl-clutching patrons aren't going to be ecstatic if they hear you talking like that."

"For a progressive city such as Boulder, they sure as hell don't like the queer guy behind the desk as it is," Ronin said, rolling his eyes. "They can deal with my language."

"Yeah, they can. And as for Bristol? We're taking things slow."

"You're engaged, not too slow."

"We can take it slow and still be engaged," Marcus said, knowing that wasn't entirely correct. But he was still figuring shit out, after all.

"Go get to your appointment in Denver. We'll be here when you get back. And I better be invited to the wedding."

Marcus pushed back from his desk entirely and stood up. "You know you will. And the guys already want you to come to our guys' night or whatever."

"Is it going to involve lifting? Because I can do that, but I'd rather go for wings. Wings sound great."

"And now I'm starving. Thank you for that."

"I try. Now, back to work. The book club's coming in today."

Ronin didn't have to elaborate. Many clubs came in, and they loved them. However, there was one book club that Marcus hated. They were rude, cranky, and demanding. And they didn't seem to like books at all. They mostly wanted to judge and to lord over them. But it wasn't like he could kick them out. Not when his bosses loved the ladies, and one of them was their cousin. So, Ronin and Marcus dealt with it. It was one of the small things that made his job not the best at times. But still worth it.

He wasn't headed home. Instead, he went to Bristol's house to pick her up. He had made this appointment down in Denver nearly a year ago and had planned to go alone. He had honestly thought Bristol would be on tour by now. Instead, she was going with him.

He tried to let that little clutch finally go away at the thought of her on tour. She was allowed to do that. It was her fucking job. Just because he felt like he was going to miss her even more now than before didn't mean he had any say in the matter. They'd figure out a plan. He had enough time off that he could visit her around the world. Or, there was such a thing as a phone. With the invention of video calling, you were never too far away from someone. At least, that's what he told himself when he got stressed out about the idea of it.

Bristol was waiting for him on her porch, and ran to the car, smiling.

"Are you ready?" she asked, slapping a kiss on his lips. He grunted, then tugged at her hair and tilted her head back as he took her mouth completely. She moaned into him, clutching his shoulders.

"Well, then. That's a hello. What for?"

"I felt like it. Got a problem with that?" he asked, raising a brow.

"No problem at all. I liked it. This is going to be fun, though. I've been with you for one tattoo, but this is going to be great."

"Well, I hope so. Getting into your cousins' shop is ridiculously difficult."

"That's because Austin is amazing. And so is Maya. But you're working with Austin today, right?"

Marcus nodded and pulled into the driveway.

"Yes, mostly because Austin's done nearly all of my other work. Maya hasn't, and you know how your cousins always fight over who gets to claim more territory."

"They joke about it. But if you let her do the iris, then that'll wipe the slate clean."

Marcus gave her a look before he got onto the highway.

"What was that look for?"

"Because you think I'm going to get a Montgomery iris," he replied, keeping any teasing out of his tone.

"You're not?" she asked, clearly insulted—though it was probably only for show.

"I may have had my mouth on your iris. Doesn't mean I'm going to get one of my own."

"That sounds far dirtier than it needed to be," she said, snorting. "But I thought you wanted one. Don't you?"

"Maybe. Not all those who marry into your family get one, do they?"

"I think nearly all of them do. I don't think my cousin Meghan's ex-husband did. Neither did Alex's ex-wife. But, you know, they weren't the best people anyway."

That was a complete understatement, but he wasn't going to dwell on that. "So, you're saying if I don't get the tattoo, we are automatically going to end up divorced?"

"No, I'm saying that the data does seem to prove that fact."

"Okay, whatever you say. I might get that tattoo. One day. But then I'm going to have to get my family names and crest somewhere on my body so my family's okay with it, too."

"Maybe all of them can get the Montgomery iris."

"You've lost your damn mind," Marcus said, laughing, and then he took her hand, and they made their way south towards Denver. Thankfully, it wasn't rush hour, it was the middle of the day during a workweek, so the drive wasn't that bad. And, thanks to the Montgomerys having a small parking lot behind their shop, parking was easy and free.

Of course, you had to work at the shop or be a Montgomery to park there, but Bristol had the connections.

"We'll go get ink today," Marcus said, getting out of the car. "But no iris."

"No matching tattoo, either. Other than the iris, because that's like a family crest, not a weird matching tattoo."

He nodded. "Yeah, you know, because a relationship's death is a matching tattoo or putting your name on me."

"We're not doing that," a woman with dark hair, tattoos along her arms, and a wicked grin said from the back door.

"Maya!" Bristol said, running toward her cousin. Maya hugged her hard, and they danced around a bit, the tough woman in boots looking like a little girl along with Bristol as they giggled.

"Seriously, though, no names."

"We promise. We were only joking."

"Good. Now, I see you're here to see my brother and not me. I get you. You're allowed to do that. But just know, once you're part of the family, you have to start alternating."

Marcus shook his head. "I don't know, Austin's done almost all of my work now."

"That is true, that means I get the rest of you." Maya winked and then wrapped her arm around Marcus and pulled him into the shop.

"Now, let's go play."

Marcus looked over his shoulder at Bristol, who clapped her hands and laughed.

The Montgomerys were indeed all crazy, and he loved the fact that he was already family.

CHAPTER 14

Bristol let her body move with the music, her bow against the strings, producing the exact notes that she wanted. Though at this point, she wasn't thinking note per note, or even looking at the pages in front of her. She had her eyes closed, and she let herself breathe into the song.

The piece wasn't one she had written but was one she was putting on her next album. It was one of age, of sorrow, but also of great love. And it was one that took every ounce of her soul, her body, and skill.

And she loved it.

Though she practiced hours per day, and had performed countless times, she knew that if she didn't keep up with it, even with all of the years of experience under her wings, she wouldn't be able to play this song.

And that was why she loved what she did. Because she was constantly learning, she was consistently adding to her repertoire and earning the love and adoration of those who enjoyed her work.

Bristol was still figuring out exactly who she needed to be and what type of artist she was going to turn into eventually, but that was why she played as she did. That was why when she was asked to play at this concert in downtown Denver, she had readily agreed because she loved what she did and wanted to do it.

It helped that she knew that those who loved her were in the audience, as well.

Marcus was there, along with his mother and father. Her parents were there, as were her brothers, and their women and Lincoln. Aaron had said that he would bring a date, although she was pretty sure he had been joking with her. He was too busy working on his projects to focus on dating. At least, that's what he had said the last time their mother had asked.

After all, all of her other baby chickens were now in a nice little row, and Aaron was the only one left.

She let all of those thoughts flow through her even as she focused on her music, on who she needed to be.

This was what she loved.

The music, the cello beneath her fingers, and between her legs.

She loved the fact that she could feel a connection to

the audience as they moved with her while she continued to play. And as she reached the last note, the one that made her catch her breath, the one that stung the backs of her eyes as she transcended into the song, she let it linger, and then there was silence.

Absolute silence.

When the first claps began, she opened her eyes and smiled.

While she loved the applause and the fact that she connected with others, despite what some may think, her favorite part was the music itself. The idea that others could listen and have their interpretation of the song was also a significant part of why she did this. But not the only piece.

She let out a breath and then set her cello aside so she could stand, bowing a bit as the audience began to cheer. She waved, trying to look into the faces under the bright lights to see those she loved, but she couldn't. She knew they were there. She had seen them before she even started, after all.

But now she was tired and wanted to go home.

She wasn't as young as she had been when she first started this life of hers. Not being in her early twenties made a big difference. But she was in shape and practiced enough that she could have probably gone for a couple of additional hours before she passed out.

However, instead of going out to a party, or dancing

the night away, she was going home with Marcus to get some sleep.

She had added this performance at the last minute, so to make sure that she was ready for it, she had practiced day in and out. To the point where the two of them hadn't been on another date since she'd first said yes to the concert. She hadn't seen her family and rarely talked to anyone. No, she had been focused on her music, to the detriment of everyone and everything else.

Perhaps she needed to change that. Because it wasn't only her now, she was an item. A duo. A couple. She had never been good at dating, so maybe she needed to find a way to be good at this.

She exited the stage, and her assistant was there to help her with her cello.

She used her assistant, Chelsea, mostly on tour, because honestly, Bristol couldn't do it all. Chelsea also helped with her social media, though Bristol tried to be herself as much as possible on there. Although Instagram was pretty much the only place she really visited anymore.

It was odd to think that in some circles, people knew her name and her music. She wasn't merely Bristol Montgomery, daughter, sister, friend, and now fiancée.

She smiled at that, and Chelsea gave her a curious look.

"Nothing, thank you for everything."

"No problem. I'll get everything ready for you, but you're all set. You can head home if you want. I know you must be tired—this sort of crept up on us."

"I know. And I know there's that cocktail party that I'm really too tired for."

"Everybody already knew you would be tired. And we made sure that it wasn't you being a diva or anything," Chelsea said, rolling her eyes.

Bristol grinned at that. "Yeah, we don't need that to be my reputation."

"You, a diva? Never," Colin said, and she stiffened. She hadn't expected that British accent. No, she had thought Colin had gone home.

Apparently, he hadn't.

Now, here he was, backstage at her event, where even her family wasn't allowed.

Of course, he had wheedled his way back here.

But others were watching, so she pasted on a smile and air-kissed his cheeks.

"I didn't know you'd be here," she said, trying not to sound accusatory.

"Of course, I'm here. You are my girl."

"Colin," she warned, still through a smile on her face.

"I just wanted to tell you that you're doing fantastic. You truly are. Look at all of this. I mean, I'm so proud of you. Look how far you've come."

Had he always been so condescending, or was she

only now noticing it? She couldn't quite believe that she had dated him for as long as she had. It didn't matter now, though, she was done with that, and she was moving on.

"Hey," a voice said from her side, and she turned, relief slamming into her.

"They let you back here," she said, throwing her arms around Marcus's waist. He held her close and then kissed the top of her head, careful of her hair and makeup. She was grateful for that because it had taken her forever to get ready for the show that morning since she was exhausted.

"Ah, the boyfriend's here."

"Fiancé, but it's good to see you, Colin. Are you playing today?" Marcus asked, keeping his arm around her waist. He didn't sound jealous at all, or even territorial. She liked that. Because she could take care of herself, and Marcus knew it.

"No, sadly, but maybe one day I'll come down and do something for them."

She knew for a fact that they hadn't asked Colin to play. Maybe because he was an asshole the last time they had. Colin was making it sound like he wouldn't lower himself to play. But there was nothing she could do about that, and now people were starting to watch. Great.

"Anyway, thanks for coming, Colin, I'm going to head home. I'm a little tired."

"I see," he said, looking into her eyes.

Asshole.

"Are you sure you're not going to come and see your fans at the cocktail party? They're going to miss you."

"No, I already told them when I signed up that I wouldn't be there for that. But I did do this at the last minute. I need to head home now, Colin, if that's okay."

"Of course, it's okay, darling. I'll go in your stead. Don't you worry."

She wanted to wrap her hands around his neck and squeeze just a little bit. She honestly didn't hate him, even though she often said she did. When they worked together, they produced beautiful music. But he was starting to annoy her, and she had a feeling it had more to do with her being tired than anything else. At least, that's what she hoped.

Others started to look at them even more, and whisper, so she rolled back her shoulders, leaned into Marcus's side, and smiled.

"Have a great night, Colin. You ready to go, Marcus?"

He squeezed her hip and nodded. "Yes, let's head home."

She didn't miss the way Colin's eyes narrowed at that word. But her hearing it? It felt amazing.

This had been a start for them. An idea of who they could be in the future when they had promised to marry one another. Now, it felt real. This could be a future. Her playing, him being there, and her finding a way to make sure he knew that she appreciated him in every way possible.

She just wasn't sure what would happen when she was gone for so long the next time.

It had all started with a promise that could have been a joke, but now it was real, and her mouth was going dry at the thought.

"Everybody's heading to your parents' house tonight. You don't have to go if you don't want to, but they wanted to give you some space here. I hope that was okay."

She pulled herself out of her thoughts at the sound of Marcus's voice. "That sounds great. I don't have to be on at my parents' house," she whispered as they made their way out of the building and to his car.

"That's what they figured. You can take off your shoes and fall asleep on the couch if you want."

"That sounds amazing. I might fall asleep on the car ride home."

"You're welcome to do that, too." He paused for a second, and she looked at him. "You're amazing. I mean, I've watched you play for what seems like my entire life, but tonight? You were transcendent."

She lost all thoughts, merely blinked at him. "Really?"

"Yes, *really*. God, Bristol. I can't believe you can do that. It doesn't make any sense to me."

She frowned, confused. "What do you mean?"

"I'm not saying this right. You were just so amazing, and watching you play, it felt like you were a whole other person. I'm glad I got to be here for it. I mean, I'm not the best at classical music, or even knowing everyone in your circles, but what I do know, I follow because I love watching you play, and because it's part of your world. You know?"

"I know. Not everybody has to know every single famous cello player or the name of the pieces I play. But you've always tried. And I've always appreciated that."

"Well, I'm going to try harder. Especially since I know you have a tour coming up."

She winced.

"Yeah, I guess we need to talk about that."

"I figured we should do the wedding after that," he said, casually.

"So, you're going to be okay that I might be gone for a while, though, right?"

"It's part of your job. We'll figure it out. I don't know exactly how, but we have time. We've always figured it out before."

And as she slid her hand into his, she let out a sigh and hoped that he was right.

Because she was falling for him, or maybe she had always had him in her heart in ways she hadn't let herself dwell on.

She just hoped that they weren't making mistakes.

That would cost them more than anyone had to give.

CHAPTER 15

*M*arcus leaned against the back of the couch and watched Bristol flail her hands as if she were trying to fly. He just shook his head and laughed.

"A birdcage?" he asked, and she sighed, flapping her hands again, and then putting her elbows to her sides before waving them even more.

The other Montgomerys started to laugh, and Marcus shook his head, confused.

"I have no idea."

"Time," Liam said, and Bristol cursed under her breath.

"We're usually much better than this."

"What the hell were you?"

"A velociraptor."

Everyone was silent for a moment, and then Marcus burst out laughing, trying to keep from falling off the couch. "You were pantomiming flying."

"I thought there was evidence that velociraptors could fly." She winced, and Marcus snorted again. His woman. He just couldn't sometimes.

"Sure, I've heard that too, but don't put it in a game of charades," Aaron said, wiping tears from his eyes.

Holland was his teammate and was currently sitting next to him, laughing so hard she indeed did fall off the couch.

"I thought you guys were the reigning champs," Arden said, looking confused.

"We usually are. Must be an off night," he said, reaching out his hand.

"Come here."

"No. You're going to laugh at me." Bristol folded her arms over her chest, but Marcus simply smiled.

"That wasn't a velociraptor, babe. And you know it. We're still going to win. We have two more rounds. And I kicked ass earlier."

"Fine. You're the reason we're good at charades. I am evil." She came to him then, and sat on his lap, even as her brothers glared at him. He wrapped his arm around her waist, not caring that other people were looking. Because this was his fiancée, people could suck it.

"Maybe you were better at charades as best friends,

rather than an engaged couple," Aaron said, and Marcus frowned as the other man went pale. "Sorry. Forget I said anything. That was fucked up."

"Yes, it was," Bristol said before sliding off of Marcus's lap to take her seat on the couch.

"It's fine," Marcus whispered, not wanting to get into a fight with any of the Montgomerys just then. He and Bristol had been a little bit on edge ever since the concert. He wasn't sure why. He wouldn't have noticed but Bristol wasn't talking with him. Oh, they were at the Montgomerys having a fun game night since they hadn't wanted to go to a bar or out in a large group. Except it was as if the two of them were drifting apart, and he didn't understand why. Maybe their game of charades was the reason for him noticing.

She wasn't talking to him about anything. She was focusing on work, but they weren't mentioning the fact that they were engaged. They had no plans other than that they would figure it out. And it was getting to the point where he felt like they were playing make-believe rather than living in a real relationship. And perhaps that was the problem. What if this was just a dream, some-thing fake to play with like a promise when they were kids? Rather than something authentic.

The fact that he didn't know the answer to that worried him.

"Okay, I guess it's my turn," Holland said, standing up.

"All right. But you're going to kick ass at this," Aaron said, clapping his hands in front of him.

"Holland, baby, you can't let Aaron beat us," Ethan said, grinning at his woman.

Marcus snorted.

"Oh, Aaron and I are going to kick your ass. Lincoln's, too. I mean, I love you both, but mama's going to win."

Marcus snorted and reached out to squeeze Bristol's knee. She smiled at him, but it didn't reach her eyes. Damn it, they needed to fucking talk. The time for figuring out exactly where they started and how they were going to make this work had long since passed. This wasn't the bright sparkle of a new relationship or whatever the fuck people called it these days, this was real, and they needed a fucking plan. No more sweeping it under the rug and pretending that they knew what they were doing. Clearly, they did not.

He kept telling himself there was no going back, but maybe there needed to be. If he didn't look back, he was terrified there would be no moving forward. And that scared him more than anything. As it should.

"Okay, get ready for me to beat your ass," Holland said.

Marcus didn't even have to look in the trio's direction to know that they were giving each other heated looks while Liam and Aaron both covered their faces with their hands, and Arden and Bristol laughed.

"I don't need to know these things," Bristol said. She looked over at Marcus. "Why aren't you wincing?"

He tried to study her face but could only see the Bristol he knew and loved. "Sorry, how dare you guys talk about charades in front of your poor baby sister."

"That's not what I meant, dork." She elbowed him in the gut, but it didn't hurt.

He knew this was only a game, but it felt like more. So, they would play, they would laugh, and he'd try to understand where exactly things with him and Bristol were going wrong.

ARDEN AND LIAM WON CHARADES. MARCUS STILL couldn't quite believe it. Sweet little Arden with her innocent little face and her quiet and broody Montgomery just happened to kick all of their asses.

"It's a sham, I tell you, a complete sham," Bristol said, tapping her foot to the beat of the music in the car.

Marcus looked over at her before turning a corner. "I don't know. I think it's always the quiet ones."

"But you're my quiet one. We always win."

"I think it's because you're competitive as fuck," Marcus said honestly.

"You're secretly competitive, too."

"I will never beat you, and I'm perfectly fine with that. However, I think Arden and Liam came to win.

"And we didn't?" she asked, her voice soft.

"I don't know. Maybe they just had a good night."

"And we had a bad one."

There was an awkward silence there, and Marcus didn't like it. They never had awkward silences. At least not until recently. What the fuck was wrong with him? Why couldn't he figure out what he wanted?

Did he want things to go back to the way they were? He didn't think so. But he needed what they had to move forward. He was tired of waiting. It felt like he'd been doing that for his entire life.

Waiting to become who he needed to be.

Waiting for Bristol to come back.

Waiting to see how she felt about him once the colored lenses of their romance and what they had promised each other fell away.

The idea that, somehow, they had been playing make-believe this entire time should have hurt, but he couldn't let it. Because if he didn't fight for what he wanted, if he didn't tell her how he felt, then what was the point? And what was the point of wanting Bristol to tell him what he wouldn't even tell her? It made him a fucking hypocrite, that's what.

They made their way back to her house.

"I'm tired. I didn't realize that playing silly games would do that to me."

"I don't think it's only the games. You've been practicing your ass off recently."

Bristol winced. "I'm sorry. I'm trying to get these last songs down for the album, then the tour is coming up, and it's all so much at once. I feel like I'm losing my mind."

Marcus moved closer and opened his arms so she could fit against his chest. She slid into his hold, wrapping her arms around his waist as she rested her head on his upper chest. She tucked into him, and he loved it.

But she'd always been there. Before he started to let his feelings change, they had always touched like this.

That was why it was so hard for him to truly discern if this was what she wanted, or if she just didn't know what else there was.

She had so much going for her, why would she want to stay home with someone who didn't like to leave the nest? He had his dreams, and he was working on them. But they didn't go to the same places that hers did. And that was only one part of the problem.

And it worried him. It truly fucking did. But he didn't know what he was supposed to do about it. Other than be here for her.

And hope to hell she was there for him.

"I'm just tired. I know it's going to get worse on the long tour, and I'm trying to juggle so much." She leaned back, looking at his face. "But I'm glad that I have you.

You know? That you're always here. No matter what. And I'm not alone."

He nodded, tucking her hair behind her ears. "Yeah. I'm glad I'm always here, too."

He hoped there wasn't any bitterness in that. Because there shouldn't be. He was far from bitter when it came to her. Because while he joked that he was always left behind, he liked where he was. He loved the fact that they had their own lives. And in the end, they always came back together.

He hadn't let himself think about what they could be for long enough that he had hidden it even from himself for all these long years.

But fuck, he loved her. Fucking loved her.

Yet why couldn't he say the words?

He was as bad as she was. Unable to say the words because he was too damn scared. What would happen once he lost her?

He didn't have the answers to that, so he didn't even broach the subject. Once again, he was that fucking asshole.

"Hey, I just realized I never gave you your birthday present," he said, trying to change the subject. And in the end, if he gave her her present, even if it didn't turn out, it was showing her a part of himself.

And as he thought about it, he wondered how the hell he had buried his head in the sand for so long. Because he knew exactly how much he loved her. Had put that into her gift.

And yet, he had told himself it was because they were friends. Because they always had each other's backs.

How idiotic was he, indeed?

"Oh, yeah. I thought your gift was yourself." She grinned, and he knew she wasn't that far off.

Because, in a way, that was the truth.

"Partially. But I'm not that egocentric."

"Well, you have a right to be sometimes. I'm just saying."

"You flatter me." He tapped her butt and then moved her into her studio.

"What are we doing in here?"

"Well, it's your gift." He had left his guitar over here the day before when he practiced with her. She had wanted someone to play with, even though he was nowhere near her skill, but she had needed someone else in the room so she could focus and let out tension. And he'd needed to do the same in terms of stress because of his work, and frankly, his feelings for her.

"Here is your gift."

Her eyes widened.

"Are you going to play for me? I love it when you play for me."

"I wrote you something. But, if you hate it, lie to me."

Tears filled her eyes, and he held back a wince.

"What?"

"You wrote me a song?" she asked, wiping her cheeks.

"Don't cry. I haven't even started playing yet. When you realize how bad I truly am, *then* you can cry."

"No, you do not get to do that, Marcus. You wrote me a song."

"You still haven't heard it yet. Give it time."

"Okay. I promise I will. I'm just so excited." She sat down on the chair in front of him as he picked up the guitar and found his way.

She was still crying as he slowly began the song, his voice deep, a little rough as he sang.

He didn't look at her. He couldn't. But he hoped the words told her what he felt. Because he wasn't sure how to do so in any other way. Music was how Bristol spoke, how she connected with the world, so maybe this would be a connection for them both. Or maybe he saw far too much into it. He honestly didn't know.

He kept singing, words about who she was, and how he felt. He had written this song before he let himself love her. Before he let himself think about who they could be together.

When he finished, he looked up to see Bristol on her knees in front of him, tears running down her cheeks as she leaned against him.

"So," he said, clearing his throat, "I guess you liked it?"

"That was the most beautiful thing I've ever heard," she said, hiccup-sobbing.

He frowned.

"No, it wasn't. But thank you for thinking so."

"Stop it," she whispered.

"Stop what?"

"Stop downplaying your talent. I know that this isn't the thing that you've always wanted to do. I know it's not your life like it is mine, but you are amazing. You put so much soul into that. Your soul. And I'm in awe."

"Really?" he said, not quite believing that. But the fact that she was crying might lend some credence to her statement.

"So, I guess I'm going to have to one-up myself for your birthday next year," he said, trying to keep his tone light.

She smiled then, her eyes bright, and then rose up on her knees so she could kiss him. He lowered his head, moving the guitar out of the way, and kissed her softly.

"I think you're going to have to work hard because that was pretty amazing."

Marcus grinned. "Well, I guess that was kind of stupid of me, wasn't it?"

Her phone buzzed, and she frowned, looking at the readout before hitting ignore.

"Who was it?" Marcus asked, worried at the look on her face.

"Nobody."

Marcus was silent for a moment, staring at her.

She rolled her eyes. "Colin. He wants to go on that tour and to write something together on my album, even though we aren't planning on it. He's annoying me, but I also know that my agent sort of wants us to work together. We sell better together, and they're throwing around the idea of making a single for charity."

She crossed her eyes, but Marcus frowned.

"You'd still work with him, then?" There wasn't jealousy sliding through him, not really, but he wasn't excited about the idea of her and Colin working so closely together either.

"It's freaking annoying, but I might have to. If it's for charity? I don't know if I could say no to that just because he sometimes annoys me."

"Only sometimes?" Marcus asked, still sitting while she was on her knees. He kind of liked that, even though he didn't say it aloud.

"Okay, a lot of the time. But, occasionally he's great. And he's a fantastic piano player. One of the best of our time, and I have to remember that when we're working together."

"Being really good at something doesn't give you an excuse to be an asshole."

"That is true. And I don't let him get away with it.

You've seen me. I tell him right to his face that he's being an asshole and that he needs to stop. And he's not always that bad. I mean, he has been a little clingy recently, but I think that's only because he assumed we were going on tour together. And now that we aren't, he's scrambling a bit."

"Scrambling?" Marcus asked, not liking the sound of that.

"Oh, he's going to get his tour settled soon, but I think he kind of assumed that I would be doing all the work for this one like I usually do."

"See? Still a fucking asshole," Marcus said.

"You're right. However, I'm not going to deal with it tonight. Tonight, I am going to stay right here for my birthday gift." Her eyes darkened, and Marcus grinned.

"Oh?" he asked.

"Oh," she said, and then her hands went to his belt.

He helped her undo his pants, slowly sliding them down a bit, and when she gripped his cock through his underwear, he swallowed hard.

"Dear God, woman. You're going to kill me."

"I promise I'll be good," she said, licking her lips.

"Okay, just don't be that good," he said, laughing.

"Never." Then she squeezed him at the base before slowly pulling him out of his boxer briefs.

When she slid her hand up and down his length, he let out a groan, tangling his fingers in her hair.

"You know, I was thinking earlier that I liked you on your knees, but I didn't want to be that guy."

Bristol looked up, laughter in her eyes. "Considering I'm about to have your dick in my mouth, you're welcome to be that guy. Remember, you're going to have to reciprocate at some point. Because I like it when you're on your knees."

"I can totally do that."

And then Marcus couldn't think anymore because her mouth was on his dick, her warmth encasing the head of him to the point that his eyes crossed, and he groaned, his hands tightening in her hair. She licked up the base, and then dove her tongue at the crease on the top, lapping up the precum.

She had one hand on his thigh, the other on his length, squeezing the base, and she couldn't swallow all of him.

Her head bobbed, her mouth warm, the suction so fucking good he knew if he weren't careful, he'd come right there down her throat.

She laughed at him, sucking and moving faster, her hands squeezing. Her other hand dug into his thigh, her nails sharp points, and he loved it, wanting more.

He was about to blow, so he pulled her off him and went down to his knees in front of her, tossing the chair back, careful not to hurt anything else in the room. His lips were on hers as she opened her mouth to speak, and he tangled his tongue with hers, forcing her head back to deepen the kiss. He slid his hand up her front, squeezing her breast, and then the other, and she arched into him, clearly wanting more. When he pulled back, she gasped.

"Marcus, I wasn't done yet."

"Yeah, you are, because I want to fuck you hard right here in your favorite place in the house. And that means I can't come down that pretty throat."

"Fine, but next time, I'm swallowing." She winked, and Marcus laughed before kissing her again and then pushing her to her back. He had her pants off in an instant, and then her shirt, too. Somehow, she was naked in front of him, and he tugged off his shirt, his pants only halfway down, but he didn't care. Because he was kneeling in front of her, his head between her thighs. He pushed up the back of her thighs so her knees were near her shoulders, and then he was lapping at her, licking, sucking. She screamed his name as he sucked on her clit, needing more. His tongue dove, and he sucked, his teeth scraping a little. And when she came, her whole body shaking, he kept eating her out, wanting her even closer to the edge.

He went up to his knees and stroked his cock, wondering where the hell he had put that condom.

Bristol looked up at him again, her hands on her breasts.

"We already took the test. We're both clean. Now, get inside me."

"Are you sure?" he asked, squeezing his dick so that he wouldn't come at the thought of being in her bare.

"I have an IUD. Now, get in me."

They had talked about this, the only thing in the future they had honestly talked about, and now they were right here, the moment everything.

He lowered himself over her, his mouth on hers, and then he plunged deep. She screamed, her legs wrapping around his waist as her inner walls tightened like a vise around his dick.

And then he moved, in and out, slowly at first, and then he was pounding inside of her, her fingernails raking down his back to the point he knew they would leave marks. He kissed her hard and then sucked on her throat, and then the valley between her breasts. He pinched at her nipples, squeezing her, and he knew he would leave little marks, like both of them liked. And when he reached between them, his thumb over her clit, she shattered, her voice hoarse as she screamed, and he pounded into her again, harder, until they were both in ecstasy, oblivion taking them.

He came with a roar, filling her up as he slammed into her once more, and then they were both shaking, holding onto one another, neither of them able to move.

He petted her, unable to do anything else, knowing that they were only denying the inevitable.

Did songs and actions matter more than words? He didn't know, because she spoke with music, she moved with it, so maybe she understood what he felt.

But he had no idea what she felt. And he was so afraid that this wasn't real. That he would wake up one day and realize that everything they'd had before had turned to ash, and what they had now was meaningless.

But he ignored that thought for a moment and let himself breathe, let himself hold her.

Because the time for decisions would come soon, but for now, all he wanted was her. And he let himself believe.

CHAPTER 16

*B*ristol looked down at her day planner and rubbed her temples. She needed more sleep, but that wasn't going to happen anytime soon. Weddings were coming up, though not hers because she and Marcus hadn't spoken about it. That should worry her, and it did a bit, but for now, she was more focused on the other weddings in the family. Plus, a few of her cousins were about to pop with their next babies, so there were baby showers, wedding showers, birthday parties, and a few of the kids were now getting older, so she wanted to be part of their lives, too.

Her whole family was growing by leaps and bounds, and she was a part of that. Only she was going to be gone for the next month at least, maybe two if her agent and the tour had their way. Two whole months away, and she wasn't going to be near Marcus.

She had done something like this before, too many times to count. But now it felt different. And it *should* feel different.

The two of them weren't talking, and it was killing her. She had thought they'd always talked about everything, but she was wrong. If they had, then maybe she would know precisely what her feelings were. She didn't, though, and she still didn't let herself face those feelings fully.

She didn't know why. They were getting married.

She looked down at her ring finger and frowned. It still didn't feel real. Like it was a joke that now had gone too far, and there was no turning back from it.

That was something she needed to fix, but she didn't know how.

However, that was going to change. Today, after her practice, Marcus was coming over, and they were going to make dinner and have a relaxing night in. She would finally tell him that she loved him.

They did this whole relationship entirely backward. And she knew that, but she was going to fix it.

Because he always did so much for her, it was her turn to do something for him. But what if he didn't love her. What if, in the end, he was only doing this because he thought it was the right thing to do. He never went back on a promise. That was Marcus. So, maybe that's why he was still in this. Oh, they had great sex. But was that because they had chemistry? Or was it because they were good at it?

She didn't have the answer to that, and it worried her.

And so, she would have to put herself out there, finally. And hope to hell that he loved her back.

And if he didn't?

She put her hand over her belly and took a deep breath. If he didn't, then they would have to go back to being friends.

Friends who knew what each other tasted like.

She knew that song, loved playing that song, how friends didn't know what each other tasted like, but maybe they could go back because she refused to lose him.

And that was totally selfish of her.

She closed her planner, rolled her shoulders back, and knew she had to get back to practice. She was having trouble with this song, and she knew it wasn't for lack of trying. No, it was because her mind was on other things.

The doorbell rang in that instant, and she frowned. No one was supposed to be here. Marcus was working, as was the rest of the family.

Maybe it was the UPS driver or something.

She went to the front door and looked through the peephole and groaned.

"Of course," she whispered, hoping he didn't hear her through the wood.

Bristol opened the door and tried to smile. "Colin, what are you doing here?"

He smiled at her and stuck his hands into his pockets. "Hey, I was driving around, trying to work out the last bit of a song, the one I told you about, and figured I might stop by."

"You were driving around Boulder and just happened to come to me?" she asked.

"Yes, but I found myself driving directly towards you, if that makes any sense."

"Maybe. I was about to get some practice in. What's up, Colin?"

"Practice? You think I can join you?"

She held back a wince. "I don't know. I'm focused at the moment."

"I'm not going to bother you. I promise. It would be good to have two people working together, right? And there's that song that our agents want to do." He quickly held up his hands as she opened her mouth to speak. "I'm not the one who brought up the idea. Yes, I want to go on a tour with you, and I know it could help us, not just you, not only me, but both of us, but the song wasn't my idea. However, it's a great one. And for charity. How can we go wrong?"

This was the Colin that she usually liked. The one that

wasn't so self-centered. He hid that part of himself a little too often.

"Okay, fine, I could use a little help, honestly."

Colin's eyes brightened. "Really?"

"Really. I'm working on this last bit of a new piece, and I have a feeling it all has to do with my brain. But I could use someone to listen and figure out where I'm holding myself back."

"Well, I'm here for you. Always, Bristol. You know that, right? I mean, I know we're not together anymore, and that's perfectly fine. But we can be friends. After all, you're moving on, getting married and shit."

She smiled, but she didn't know where he was going with this.

"I am getting married. It's going to be kind of amazing."

"Oh, yeah. Totally. Is he going to go on tour with you? Or are you going to have to deal with not seeing each other for long periods? You know how lonely it can get out there. Even with everybody surrounding you, you need your core people. What are you going to do?" They were walking towards her back studio and practice area, and she frowned, not liking that his thoughts were going along the same path as hers. She didn't know if he had an ulterior motive, but it was Colin, so perhaps he did.

"We're still working on that. Everything's still new."

"I'll say. Didn't even realize you were dating, and

suddenly, you're getting married. I haven't seen the full announcement yet either, you know, on social media. You guys just keeping it close?"

She frowned as she sat down in her chair, rolled her shoulders back, and got ready to pick up her cello.

"I don't put personal things on social media. It's all about work, and sometimes, me practicing the cello from the house. That's all the Instagram they get from me."

"Well, you're Bristol Montgomery. People care about you. They care about your personal life, even if you think you're hiding it."

She frowned again, settling her cello between her legs. "I don't think I'm hiding it. I know I am. They don't need every part of me. Nobody does." Except for Marcus, but she didn't say that. It was understood. At least, she hoped so.

"Anyway, where are you having trouble? Show it to me. Let me listen."

She settled in and picked up her bow, frowning. "The world doesn't need to know everything. I'm only a cello player."

"No, you're *the* cello player. The face of our generation."

"That's laying it on a little thick," she said dryly.

Colin shrugged, even as he sat down at the small piano she had in the corner. It had been a gift for herself when she wanted to learn the instrument thoroughly.

Colin had been the one to push her at it, and honestly, she hadn't been too worried about that. She had wanted to play, as well. Wanted to make sure that she had more than just one talent up her sleeve.

"I want to be the best. I don't want to simply be another piano player. I want to be the one that people think of. I want to be the one that those outside our community know. And if that makes me an arrogant asshole, then fine. People will have to get used to it."

She shook her head. "There has to be a middle ground. I want to be the best at what I do, but I don't want to be the best in terms of putting other people down along the way."

"I don't think you have to do that. But what do I know? I'm a simple piano player."

She snorted. "You just spent how long explaining to me that you want to be the best, and you already think you are. There's nothing simple about you."

"You say the sweetest things," he said, winking at her. "Now, get to it. I want to hear you play."

She nodded and closed her eyes, took another breath, and then began to play, not needing to see the music for this first part. She had the whole thing memorized, but that didn't matter. When she got to a specific part, she would have to open her eyes and look. She flowed with it, knowing Colin was in the room but ignoring him. It was all about her and the music and what she needed to breathe with, but when she got to the part she kept slipping up on, she opened her eyes and focused on the notes in front of her, ensuring that her fingers were in the right places, by feel, by sound, and by a simple sense of knowing. When she finished, she let out a deep breath, any tension she'd had long gone thanks to the music.

She looked up at Colin, who was frowning at her, his eyes narrowed, intense.

"Horrible, right?"

"On the contrary. You're quite astonishing. But I see that one piece. And I feel like you're flowing toward a crescendo and then the music changes at that one moment, but it's not your fingers or the way that you're putting pressure on them. You're right, it is in your head."

"See? And you can't just change that. I don't know what to do other than scream at it and tell myself I'm going to be fine. But now I have this mental block in my head, and I can't get over it."

"That song has piano on it, do you have your iPad with you?"

She nodded and handed it over to him, unlocking it. He did a search and then groaned.

"I knew I had this. Okay, what if I play with you, at least the harmony line, and we can see what happens? Maybe at that part, if you let go and have fun with it, you'll get through your mental block."

"You think that's going to happen?"

"It could."

"Okay, let's try," she said, and then let out a breath before she got into position.

The two of them laughed, playing decently well the first time, and Colin shook his head.

"Okay, now that we've got that crap out of our system, let's do this again. We can do it."

"So you say, I feel like I'm just getting worse."

"This is practice. You're not supposed to be amazing each time."

"That is so not something that you would usually say," she said, rolling her neck.

"Maybe, but I'm attempting to be humble. You know, trying it on for size."

"Whatever."

She knew this Colin wouldn't always be here. He was still happy and smiley and helpful when he was getting what he wanted.

She was aware of that and knew that because she couldn't completely cut him out of her professional life, she could be civil. And just because he annoyed her sometimes and was a bit of a dick at other times, didn't mean that she had to grit her teeth every second of every day.

This version of Colin was easy to get along with, and as they worked for a few hours on the piece, something he didn't even need to do, she hoped this version of him was here to stay, even though she knew that wouldn't happen.

The music flowed through her on their final practice, and she skimmed over a part that always tripped her up, and then she was there, living in the moment, just breathing through the music. At the final notes, she set her cello down as well as the bow and stood up, clapping. "Fuck, yeah. That's how you do it."

Colin stood up with her, picked her up by the hips, and slung her around.

She pushed at him, rolling her eyes. "I told you, you could do it. Now, who's the best teacher?"

"That would be me," she said, laughing. "Seriously, though, thank you. I needed to get out of my head, and playing with someone else really helped."

Just like when she played with Marcus, even though he said that he wasn't good enough, he was. She loved playing with him, and it helped work out any kinks she had. Plus, she loved being next to him. She couldn't wait for him to come over later so she could tell him that to his face.

"You're amazing." And then Colin's hand was on her face, and his lips were on hers.

It took her a moment to realize what the fuck was happening. She was on a high from playing and hadn't even realized that Colin's lips were on hers or that it wasn't Marcus.

She felt oily, but she didn't want to make a big deal out of it, didn't want to make him angry, or worse. So, she pushed him away and laughed.

"Stop it," she said.

"Yeah, let's not do that," a voice said from the door. She turned, noticing for the first time that they weren't alone. And like before, when he'd been in the doorway, and Colin's hands were on her, he looked pissed.

"Marcus," she whispered.

She had a feeling it wasn't going to be easy to explain this time.

It might not be her fault, but it looked like she had hurt him. And she couldn't fix that.

CHAPTER 17

*M*arcus did his best not to believe his first impression. He honest to God knew that Bristol wouldn't cheat on him.

This had Colin and his fucking asshole face all over it.

But the fact that Colin's hands were still on Bristol's face, and her lips were all swollen and shit meant that it was tough for him not to want to murder someone just then.

What did he know? He was only the fiancé that she didn't fucking love. Bristol pushed Colin off her, and Marcus fisted his hands at his sides. He wasn't a violent man, and he wasn't going to turn into one.

"Marcus, I didn't realize it was so late. We have our date tonight."

"Seems like," he said, his voice neutral.

"Hello there," Colin said, that fucking British accent annoying Marcus to no end. It was like the other man laid it on thick when he was trying to needle him. And that was probably true. Colin was a fucking asshole.

"Colin came by, and I was working, having trouble with that song I talked about. And then we worked together on it, but I finally got it. Finally. That's great, right?"

Marcus nodded. "Sounds great."

Colin leaned forward, his eyes bright. "And I guess we got caught up in the moment. You know, music does that. I mean, that's what happens when two artists get together. Sometimes, the music just overwhelms us."

"Colin," Bristol snapped. "The music may have gotten into you, but not me. You ever do that again, I'm going to knee you in the dick."

Marcus watched Colin's eyes narrow into daggers, but thankfully, the asshole simply shrugged and put on that fake smile of his. "Sorry about that, love. I guess I did get into the mood."

"Don't call me *love*. You go all fake British even though you're actually from the UK when you say that."

The other man waved it off. "Perhaps. Anyway, it seems you have a bit of a mess to clean up. Sorry for my involvement. Now, I hope we'll talk soon about the song?"

"Maybe. I don't know. You need to go, Colin."

Marcus watched the other man leave, and let Bristol stand up for herself. Because he never stepped in for that. He wasn't going to beat some guy's ass just because he could. Even though he fucking wanted to.

"I'm so sorry about that."

"The kiss? Or me catching it," Marcus asked, unable to help himself.

Bristol's eyes widened, and she stepped forward, her hand out, but she stopped at the look on his face.

At least that's why he thought she stopped. For all he knew, she was just done. Maybe he was, too.

"Colin kissed me. I did not want it. I was pushing him away. You saw that."

"And yet you keep letting him into your house?"

"Because I work with him. And he did help me. But I do know that if I have to work with him again, it'll be at a public studio, not alone with him. He's too much. I'm sorry, Marcus. I didn't mean for that to happen."

"No, you're right. You can't control him." Marcus let out a breath and then started to pace. "It's seriously not your fault. I'm not angry about that. Are you okay, though?" he asked, finally getting through the sludge that was his brain and trying not to act like an asshole.

"I'm okay." She paused. "I mean, as long as you're okay. Marcus, talk to me. What did I do?"

He sighed, trying to get his thoughts in order.

"You haven't done anything, Bristol."

He paused. "Maybe that's the problem. We haven't done a fucking thing."

Her eyes widened, and she took a step back. "What do you mean?"

"What are we doing? We're only playing at this, right?"

"No, we're not. We made a promise."

"Fuck that promise."

Her eyes widened, but she didn't say anything. Good. Because he wasn't sure what he would do if she tried to say anything. He didn't know if he'd believe it. He barely believed himself.

"What the fuck are we doing?" he asked again. "We're not...whatever we're doing, it's not going right. We barely talk, we hang out with others, and they're so scared of breaking what we had that they constantly don't mention it. It's the elephant in the room, and it's fucking killing me. What the fuck are we doing?"

"We're going to be married," she whispered.

"Yeah, that's not the right answer. If it was the right answer, you wouldn't sound so nervous about it."

"Marcus."

"No, don't. We made that promise because we were scared. And I get it. You were leaving, and I was staying behind. But that's always going to be the case. You are always going to go, and I will always be here. I'm never going to be like Colin. I'm never going to travel with you and see the world and be the type of guy you need."

"Stop it. You know that's not what I want. Colin isn't what I want. You are."

"Are you sure? Or are you just scared of backing down? This is what we have now."

"Marcus."

"Stop saying my name like that. You know it's not going to help anything."

"You're scaring me, that's why I keep saying your name. I don't know what else to do."

"I don't know either, but this isn't working. We never talk. We used to talk about everything, but even as I say that, I know it's not true. The past ten years, we purposely ignored the fact that we made a promise that seemed silly. Nobody would ever fucking do it, but suddenly, we're not backing down because Andie overheard us? What kind of fucking start to a relationship is that? I gave you a ring, one that I thought you would love, but I didn't tell you what I feel, and you're not telling me what you feel."

She was so silent. He knew that the hollow sound he heard pinging around inside him was his heart breaking. But he didn't let himself feel anything. He didn't have time for that. Not if he wanted to salvage whatever they had.

"I don't want to lose you. You're my best friend, and we rushed into this way too quickly."

"You're right, we did."

Another dagger.

"And I don't want to lose you," he repeated. "But I can't have you. You don't love me, Bristol."

She opened her mouth to speak, her eyes wide, filling with tears, but he shook his head.

"You don't love me," he repeated. "And I don't want to lose the friend I had, so I'm going to walk away right now. And then maybe, one day, we can get back to what we had, but I don't know. Because I'm not the guy you need. I'm not the one you want. I'm not saying it's Colin because we both know that's not it either. But I can't be the man you turn to when you're so afraid to look to the future. And I don't want you to be that for me either." He added the last part even though he knew it was a lie. She was his future. He fucking loved her. But he wasn't going to lay himself bare. Man, it would only make it harder for her to walk away.

"I love you," she whispered.

"But what kind of love, Bristol?" he asked, his voice raw. "You need so much more than I can give you, I think. So, you go. You be the person that I always knew you could be. And I'm going to be myself here. In Boulder. Never leaving. Because my world is here, while you have the rest of the world in your hands. And I don't think I'm the right guy for you."

Then he turned and left, leaving part of himself behind.

He didn't know if he was doing the right thing, and as soon as he said the words, he knew they were probably wrong. But like he'd said before, there was no going back. And wanting something from Bristol wasn't going to make it happen. So, he left, knowing he was making a mistake. But hell, it was what he was fucking good at, wasn't it?

CHAPTER 18

*B*ristol pulled her hair back and narrowed her eyes at the dark circles that lay under them. She hadn't slept the night before, and that was her fault.

All of this was her fault.

She had let herself believe in something that wasn't quite real. How could it have been real when she hadn't voiced her true feelings? When she had been so scared to hear what Marcus had within him that she hadn't listened to him.

This was something she would have to figure out, but she still didn't know how, wasn't sure if she ever would.

She brought out her concealer and covered her dark circles and then added some powder and a little mascara. The mascara would wash away later if she started to cry again, but that was fine. She would add more layers.

Anything to shield herself from what she was truly feeling. Because if she let herself dive deep beneath the layers, she'd find herself broken, a hollow husk of the woman she thought she was.

She hadn't wanted to lose her best friend, the man she had grown to love, and so she had created this fairytale where no one needed to ask hard questions, and everything would be fine.

Only that wasn't how the real world worked. She had broken something precious because she had been so afraid to lose it to begin with.

And there was no going back. How could she have thought there could be.

Her heart ached, and she rubbed a fist over her chest, wondering when she was going to feel whole again.

She knew the answer had to be never. How could she feel truly whole when she didn't have Marcus by her side?

There would be no going back to him being her best friend and her trying to live up to who he was to her. There would be no going back to smiles and sly innuendos.

There would be no going back to him being part of her family and vice versa.

She was never going to be a Stearn. He was never going to be a Montgomery.

And all because she couldn't tell him that she loved him.

Because he couldn't love her back.

And, because seeing her with Colin had brought that all to the forefront.

Hand fisted, nails digging into her palm, she did her best to let out a slow breath.

She shouldn't have let Colin into her house. Oh, she knew that Marcus hadn't honestly thought she had cheated on him. He would never feel like that, but the fact that she hadn't pushed Colin away immediately or more forcefully? Maybe she deserved that.

No, that wasn't right.

She had done nothing to make Colin do what he did, and she knew Marcus knew that. At least, she hoped.

But maybe seeing the tableau had forced Marcus to see what they didn't have.

What they had was a fake fairy tale where they could sleep together and pretend like everything was fine, like they weren't going to ruin everything they'd ever had.

"Great job, Bristol," she said, swallowing hard. She wasn't going to cry again, but she felt like she needed to.

She needed to practice, her tour was coming up. She didn't want to go out of town, didn't want to leave the house. She had ignored calls from her family, from everybody. All she wanted to do was hide under her blankets and pretend that everything was okay when it actually wasn't.

The doorbell rang, and she froze, her heart leaping into her throat.

"Marcus?" she asked, her voice a whisper.

But it wasn't going to be him. How could it be? Not when he had said that he needed space. And being near each other would never be the right amount of space.

She licked her lips and made her way to the door and looked through the peephole.

It wasn't Marcus, but thank God it wasn't Colin either.

"Let us in, Bristol. We have keys, too."

Bristol closed her eyes at the sound of Holland's voice, and then let out a breath.

"Please, Bristol. Something's wrong."

That was Arden.

"I don't know if breaking and entering is the best way to go about this, but I'll do it if I have to."

Madison.

And just like that, Bristol wasn't completely alone.

She opened the door, knowing she didn't want to see anyone, but realizing she didn't have a choice.

"Hey," Arden said and reached in for a hug. "I know you may not want a hug or people right now, because we have no idea what's going on, but you're not answering your phone, nor are you answering your emails or anything. So, we are here. Talk to us."

They made their way inside, and Bristol let the tears fall, knowing there went her mascara and any concealer she had just put on.

"Oh, honey," Holland said, bringing her in for a hug. Madison went to her other side, and then Bristol was there, too, and the four of them stood together as Bristol sobbed into their arms, wondering how this had happened.

Because she hadn't thought of the consequences, that's how.

Imagine that.

"Marcus ended it," she said, trying to breathe.

"He did?" Arden asked, her voice low.

Bristol looked around them and knew she had to tell the truth. There was no point in trying to make it sound any better than it was.

"It's a long story," she said honestly.

Madison nodded. "They usually are. But we're here. Promise."

Bristol let out a breath. "Marcus and I made a plan when I turned twenty that ten years from then, on my thirtieth birthday, if neither of us was married, we'd marry each other."

The faces on the women that she adored were comical at best. Wide eyes, mouths agape, and a lot of blinking.

Well, she shouldn't have been surprised.

"Really?" Madison asked. "I would have said that's brilliant, but oh God, I'm sorry, Bristol."

"Yeah, I thought it was a brilliant idea, too," she said honestly. "I thought we were making it work. And so, we decided somehow to be engaged but start dating at the same time. We didn't really talk about it, and that was the problem. And now, Marcus doesn't really know how I feel about him, and I don't know what I feel about him truly because I won't let myself actually feel anything, and...here we are." She explained in more detail about everything that had happened, and the girls listened, nodding along, holding her hands, rubbing her back.

The tears fell again, but there was nothing she could do about that. She was just going to look like death for a while now.

The four of them sat in her living room and talked about nothing. She didn't honestly think any of them would have answers for her, other than that it took time, and maybe this wasn't the end.

"You have to talk to him," Arden said honestly.

Bristol nodded. "I know I do. I don't want him to hate me." She laughed, even though it was a little watery. "Which is the most self-centered thing ever because he doesn't know how I feel about him, and that's horrible. We need to talk, and we need to figure this out. Because even if we don't go through with the engagement, I can't lose him."

"You guys have a foundation that is solid and steady, you may be a little shaky right now, but that comes from lack of communication." Holland leaned forward and squeezed her hands. "I'm in a relationship with two men. There are multiple relationships within our triad. Communication is the only way we make it work. So, you have to do the same with Marcus. I know it's scary because you don't know what he's going to think, what he's going to say. But that's part of being in a relationship. You don't know, and you have to put yourself out there so you can find out. It's so scary, but you are one of the strongest people I know, Bristol. You can do this."

Bristol wiped her face. "Well, you guys sure do believe in me more than I believe in myself."

"And that's the case for most people," Madison said. She shrugged when everyone looked at her. "I pretty much have no self-esteem, but I can tell you that I'm working on it. And I hope you are, too. Now, breathe, and know that this is going to suck for a little while, but you guys are going to figure this out. You need to talk to him."

"I know. It's stupid that we aren't. It's ridiculous. But I thought it was working. I was wrong."

"It was working, we all saw it," Arden said, her voice

soft. "However, in order for it to continue working, you need that pesky little thing called communication."

"I know," Bristol said, and the four of them talked some more before they all had to go off to their respective jobs and lives, leaving Bristol alone again. But not without hugs first, and threats of moving in if Bristol didn't get herself together and start living again. These women loved her, and she loved them right back. Even Madison, who was new to her life, but had already taken a strong hold on her heart.

The same heart that was shaky at the moment because she didn't know what was going to happen with Marcus. But she needed to figure it out.

She had to.

Bristol went through the motions of washing her face then applying a little concealer and mascara once more. No one was going to look at her, but she needed that for herself. Armor so she could formulate a plan in words for Marcus. Because she was going to fight for him, she was going to say the things that she hadn't said before. And to do that, she needed a detailed list and a plan.

That might sound silly to anyone else, but it worked for her. And others would have to deal with it.

She thought about going back to her studio, working in there, but, instead, she brought out her notebook and started to make that list.

The doorbell rang, and she frowned. She didn't think

it was one of the girls again, but maybe it was one of her brothers. After all, she meddled in their lives enough. It was only right that they do the same for her.

Bristol made her way to the door, looked out the peephole, and froze.

Hell. She had hoped it would be Marcus. Anyone other than who was on the other side of the door. She could ignore it. Keep the door locked and not open it at all. However, that would only be hiding from some of her problems. And she couldn't hide from Colin forever, not when she had to make sure that he got it through his head that he wasn't allowed to touch her like that again. And frankly, she wasn't sure she wanted to work with him in the future. Not only because he sometimes didn't understand boundaries, but also because every time she worked with him going forward, she would think of the look on Marcus's face. And she never wanted to think of that look again.

She opened the door but kept it cracked only a little so she could look at him.

"Colin, it's really not a good time. You should have called ahead."

"I'm here to check on you. You weren't answering your phone."

For a reason, but she didn't say that. After all, she hadn't been answering her phone for anybody.

"I'm busy, Colin. I'm sorry. I'll have to talk to you later."

"Let me in. I want to apologize."

"Colin, just go."

He put his hand on the door and pushed his way in, surprising her. He was much bigger than her, much stronger, something she really hadn't noticed until now.

She staggered back, and Colin moved in, closing the door behind him and locking it. The sound echoed in the room, and she swallowed hard, her whole body shaking.

"What the hell? I didn't say you could come in."

"We need to talk. Get this out in the open. Let's figure this out."

"There's nothing to figure out. You need to go. You're not welcome here right now."

"We can fix that."

"I should rephrase my statement. You're not welcome here...ever. Get out."

Her phone was in her studio, and she didn't have a house phone. Now, she regretted the fact that she didn't carry her cell with her everywhere.

"We need to talk."

"You need to go," she said, taking a step back towards her studio. Colin moved with her, and she froze.

There was something off about him today. Something she couldn't quite figure out.

He was scaring her, and that worried her.

"No, we're going to talk this out. You and me. Just like it's always been."

He walked around her.

"You're not with him? He's not here?"

"That's none of your concern. Go." She made to move around him to get to the door, but he gripped her arm tight.

She pulled, but he was stronger. His fingers dug into her flesh, and her heart raced, her breath catching in her throat.

"You need to go." She tried to keep her voice strong, but it was no use, the shake was coming out anyway.

"Bristol, we've been together for years. You and me. You can't simply toss it away now that you have someone else. I understand that he's special to you. But what about us? What about what we had? You and I? We could take over the world together. Never forget that. Never forget who I am for you." His hand squeezed even harder, and she let out a yelping sound, trying to move away.

"Let go of me," she rasped.

"I'm not going to hurt you, Bristol. But we need to talk."

"We're done. We've been done. I'm not doing this. You need to go."

"You can't do this to me!"

Bristol froze, the terror slamming through her like a wave of nausea.

"Colin. Please let go of me." She tried to make her voice sound steady, but it was anything but.

"Why? Why should I let go of you? You just don't understand." He shook her, and she tried to get away, but he put his free hand on her other arm, squeezing even harder. He was far enough away, his muscles stretched tight, that she couldn't kick at him. She couldn't get away.

She struggled, but he held her closer and tighter.

"You can't just not do the tour with me. Not do the song. I have done everything for you. I have helped you get where you are, and this is how you repay me? With disloyalty?" He shook her again, and she bit her tongue.

"Colin. Please stop."

"I'll tell you exactly where you need to be. By my side. With me. Every time. You don't get to change your mind because you found someone new. You don't get to leave me after everything I've done to make sure you're the person you need to be. I'm the one who made your career. You were nothing."

She had comebacks to that, things she wanted to say, but she knew if she told him the actual facts, he would only get angrier, so she tried to calm him down, even as her heart raced so fast she was afraid it would burst.

"Colin. We can talk this out. But please, just let me go."

"You think you can soothe me? You don't fucking know me at all, do you?"

The slap across her face startled her, and she blinked, and then she was on the floor, Colin throwing her so hard that her head hit first, and she saw stars. She tried to get up, attempted to shake her head, but she couldn't. And then he was on top of her, and she panicked, wondering what the hell was happening, how this could happen.

He pushed her down more, his fingers digging into her flesh again. She kicked out, kneeing him in the crotch. He screamed, and she pushed him off her, crawling in the direction of her phone.

He was blocking the door, but if she could get to a window or her phone, she could stop this. She could lock herself in her room, and everything would be okay. He grabbed her ankle and pulled her towards him, and she fell on her face, but she kept scrambling, kept trying to get away. She kicked at him again, this time hitting his face. The sound of her heel against his nose made a crunch, and blood splattered across the room.

He howled in rage. "You bitch," he screamed, and then he moved on her again, but this time she was faster and was able to get away. She kicked, and she screamed, raking her nails down his face. His nose was already broken, blood flowing, and she left another mark, but she wasn't able to do it again. Because he pushed her, punching her right in the stomach.

"How dare you? How fucking dare you?"

His hands went to her neck, but she kicked him once more, this time right in the junk again.

And then, she was falling, and she hadn't seen the flash of silver until it was too late.

A searing pain slid up her side, and she gasped, blinking as tears filled her eyes. She looked down at her side, as blood gushed from a wound. She put her hands over the cut as she fell fully to the floor, trying to stop the bleeding. But the hot, viscous liquid seeped through her fingers, and she cried out, wondering how the hell this had happened.

She looked up at Colin, who stood there, his chest heaving as he looked down at her, a bloody pair of scissors in his hand.

"You shouldn't have done that. We had everything. And now, you've ruined it."

She had one hand outstretched, her energy fading, and as he put his booted foot over her fingers, she screamed.

"Your precious fingers. What would happen if I broke them? You would never be able to play the cello again."

"Colin, please."

"You had your time for begging. Now, you're nothing."

But then he looked at her again, tilted his head, and moved his foot.

Her hands were safe, but as her blood pooled around her, she knew *she* wasn't safe.

She blinked, trying to focus, but then Colin was gone, the door left open, and she knew she needed to crawl. Needed to get to a phone. She had to do something.

Because she didn't want to die, but as her blood rushed out of her, her hands shaking, she was afraid that she wouldn't be strong enough.

She got to her knees and slowly crawled towards her phone, ignoring her aches and screams as each tug opened her wound even more.

Her hand slid over the cell, her blood making it hard for her to even unlock it.

And as she dialed 911 with shaky fingers, she lay there, the device next to her face, and hoped to hell she wasn't too late.

CHAPTER 19

*M*arcus growled and hit the punching bag again. And again. And again. One jab, and then a left cross. And a right cross. Then another jab.

"Okay, I think I'm going to need a break," Ronin said, shaking out his hands after he'd let go of the bag. Marcus shook out his own fists and frowned. "I wasn't hitting that hard."

"Yes. You were." Ronin raised both brows. "You want to talk about what's going on?"

Marcus shook his head. "Not really."

"Well, you're not really going to have a choice if you don't talk soon. This isn't like *Captain America*, where you're allowed to burst those bags. We're at a public gym."

It was the middle of the weekend, and they were

pretty much the only two people in the place, but Ronin was right. Marcus shouldn't be breaking shit.

"I don't want to talk about it," he said after a moment.

"You're going to have to. Mostly because I don't think it's healthy for you to bottle it all up."

Marcus looked pointedly at Ronin, who gave a shrug.

"I know I'm a hypocrite. However, we're not talking about me. You're the one going through a crisis. And I have a feeling it has to do with Bristol because you're all growly and you turned off your damn phone. You never turn off your phone in case your family or she needs you."

"Come on. I've had enough. I'm done. Or I guess I will actually break something if I keep going like this."

"Good. Well, we'll get a beer or something. I don't know. Anything to get your mind off whatever the fuck is going on."

One of the older men next to them narrowed his eyes at Ronin's language, but Marcus just rolled his eyes. He was a little tired of having to defend himself when he really didn't have a defense. And cursing when they were at a gym was something the guy would have to deal with. Plus, it wasn't like Ronin had screamed it or anything.

"Yeah, I could use a beer. Or something stronger."

Ronin's brows rose.

"Well, that's not good. You don't usually drink the hard stuff."

"I can start now."

"Is it Bristol?"

They were in the locker room now, changing, and Marcus sighed. "I think it's over."

Ronin cursed. "Over-over?"

"I don't know what we're going to be able to get back to, but yeah, I ended it."

Ronin was quiet for long enough that Marcus was afraid the other man had left.

He turned.

"You're the one who ended it?"

Marcus nodded. "Yeah. I had to. It was inevitable."

"Are you an idiot?" Ronin asked.

"That's not very helpful." His gut ached, and he felt like he hadn't slept in years, but hell, hearing Ronin agreeing with him about his stupid choices wasn't what he wanted to hear.

"No, I guess it's not very helpful. I thought you loved her. What happened?"

Marcus shrugged. "Long story."

"You can tell me that story later after we get back from the hospital," a voice said from behind them, and Marcus turned on his heel to see Aaron standing there, a glower on his face.

"Hospital? What do you mean?" tension gripped him, and Marcus moved forward.

"Maybe you need to turn on your fucking phone."

Marcus had never seen Aaron look like he did right now. Seriously, Aaron was the easiest-going and most laid-back guy Marcus knew. Right then, though, it looked like he wanted to rip the roof off the building, or Marcus's head right from his body.

"What's going on?" Marcus asked, pulling his shirt over his head and then putting on his shoes.

"That asshole attacked Bristol. She's in the hospital." Aaron swallowed hard, his hands shaking as he fisted them at his sides even as Marcus's entire body seized.

Bristol.

Hospital.

My God.

Aaron continued. "We've got to go. Your family told me you were here. It's the only way I found you. But I've wasted enough time trying to find your ass when I don't even think you need to be there."

"Colin? What the fuck did he do to her?"

"I don't know all the details, but she almost bled out on her floor, and nobody was there for her. We weren't there because we were giving her space. And you weren't there because, apparently, you're too good for her. So, fuck you."

And then Aaron was gone, and Marcus was grabbing his bag, following after him.

"Shit, let me know what's happening," Ronin called

from behind him, and Marcus nodded, leaving the other man behind.

He couldn't breathe, couldn't do anything. His hands were shaking, and he swallowed hard, trying to catch his breath.

"Fuck, Jesus Christ. Is she going to be okay? She has to be okay."

"I don't know. Liam's texted me updates, but they're waiting for her to get back from surgery. *Surgery.* He fucking stabbed her."

Aaron started breathing hard, and Marcus moved forward, nearly tripping over his own two feet, then put his hands on the other man's shoulders. "Did they find Colin?" If they hadn't, he'd find the asshole himself and kill him. Right then and there. He didn't care. He'd. Kill. Him.

"Get your hands off me." Aaron spat the words, and Marcus let his hands drop. Others were watching now, but Aaron waved them off while Marcus did the same. They let them be, and then it was only the two of them standing in a parking lot, Ronin coming in after them.

"Don't do this," Ronin said, putting himself between them. "Don't start fighting. You guys are friends. Family."

"You don't even know us," Aaron grumbled, but there was fear in his voice, and that's why the man was lashing out. And Marcus let him. He deserved all of this. And more.

"I need to get to the hospital for my sister. She would want you there, even if I don't know what the hell is going on between the two of you. My mom wants you there, so I came to find you. Everyone else has their family with them, and I was the only one left that could get away. I just needed to breathe." Aaron's eyes went glassy, and Marcus cursed under his breath.

"Can you drive?" Marcus wasn't sure how he was reasonable at all right now, but he kept himself together for Aaron.

And for Bristol.

"Yeah, that I can. Because if I get hurt on my way to her, she'll kick my ass." They both laughed, but there was no feeling in it.

"I'll follow you. I'll get there."

"Keep me updated," Ronin said, and Marcus remembered that his friend was even there, making sure that he and Aaron didn't beat the shit out of each other because there was no other outlet.

Marcus nodded and then went to his car and followed Aaron to the hospital. His hands gripped the steering wheel so tightly that he knew he would be sore later, and he was frankly surprised that the whole wheel didn't pop right off the column.

He found parking, a little bit away from Aaron, and made his way through the doors, and then through the maze of a hospital to where the waiting room was.

The rest of the Montgomerys were there, waiting. Even his mother and father were there, though his sisters and their husbands weren't.

He looked at the Montgomerys, and then went straight to his mother, too chickenshit to turn and face Bristol's family.

"Mom."

"Oh, baby, they found you. Your sisters and their husbands wanted to be here, but we didn't let them, mostly because we knew we'd pretty much take over the place." She let out a wobbly smile, and he hugged her tightly, taking in her scent and rubbing her back.

"Are you sure you should be in here?" His voice was soft, but he still worried about his mom. She'd been in and out of hospitals for years, and he hated the idea that she was back here.

"Being in a hospital waiting room isn't going to bring all the memories back. I'm healthy. And if I get tired, your father will take me home. But Bristol is my little girl, too. I need her to be okay." She squeezed his hand, even as his dad put his arm around her shoulders and helped her to sit down again.

"I'll watch her, son. You go take care of your other family. I'll make sure your mother's safe."

He met his father's gaze and saw worry there, but also saw the strength that he knew he'd need.

He couldn't breathe, couldn't think.

Bristol had to be okay.

He moved to the chair next to where Bristol's mom sat, and she looked up, tears streaming down her face.

"My daughter is so strong, and I'm glad that you're here. We couldn't get ahold of you. We were worried."

He lowered his head. "I'm sorry. I had my phone off. Never again."

Bristol's father stood up and squeezed his shoulder. "It's okay. It happens. We knew Aaron would find you." He looked over at his son. "Right?"

"Right. I found him. Any news on Bristol?"

"We're waiting to hear from the doctor. She should be out of surgery soon." Marcus looked over at Ethan, who had spoken, the other man's gaze on the clock. Lincoln and Holland sat on either side of him, their hands clutching his. They didn't speak, but they leaned into Ethan as if giving him their combined strength.

Madison was at Lincoln's side, her hand in his other, squeezing tightly.

Marcus knew that Madison and Bristol had started to become close over time, and the fact that Madison was here only reminded him how much Bristol had waiting for her.

She had to be okay.

He kept repeating that mantra as if he could will it to happen.

"What happened?" Marcus asked and looked at the doorway as another person walked in.

"That's my question, as well," Zia asked, her purple hair pulled back from her face in a messy bun. She was pale, her ink stark against her skin, and Mrs. Montgomery stood up and went over to Bristol's ex, holding her close.

"I'm glad you're here, darling. All of Bristol's family's here now. That's good."

"What happened?" Zia asked again, and Marcus looked at Liam, saw the other man's jaw tighten.

"We don't know much. Colin got into her home and attacked her. We don't know what happened, but Bristol fought back. Colin has scratch marks on his face and a broken nose and a few bruises."

His girl fought back. Of course, she did. Only she shouldn't have had to in the first place. Marcus should have been there. "They got the bastard?"

"Yeah, he was sitting in his fucking car in her driveway, muttering to himself, trying to clean up the blood when the police came." Liam spit out a curse, and Marcus let out a deep breath, trying to calm his racing heart.

"Who called the cops?"

"She did," Arden said softly. "The girls and I were just there, checking up on her after…" She moved her gaze from him, and Marcus cursed.

"Checking up on her after me," he said softly.

Arden looked reluctant to answer but finally nodded. "Yes, but she was okay. I guess he came after we left. And he didn't leave. I don't know what's going to happen to him, but the cops have him now."

"But he hurt her pretty badly," Liam said softly.

"What did he do?" Marcus asked, his voice low.

"He attacked her, hit her, and then stabbed her with some scissors."

"Fuck," Marcus whispered.

"Bristol told the cops everything when they got there. That's how we know what we do."

"And she was awake then?" Marcus asked.

"Yeah, and then she passed out because of blood loss or shock or something," Arden said. "I don't know. I've been in hospitals enough, you'd think I'd know everything, but I don't."

"Are your brothers coming?" Marcus asked suddenly, remembering that Arden's brothers were constantly in the hospital with her, the protective Brady brothers who were always there.

"I had to warn them off. But they may take turns if somebody needs a rest."

She was looking at her future in-laws, and Marcus understood.

Her siblings would ensure that Bristol's parents got to rest, probably the same as his family.

Bristol's siblings would be there, as would Marcus. Because he needed to make sure she was okay.

"Can I talk to you for a second?" Liam asked, his voice low. Everyone quieted, and Marcus's shoulders tightened.

"Yeah. You can."

After all, he deserved the fist to his face if that's how this ended up.

"Liam," his father said, his voice a barked order.

"It's fine. Only talking. Promise."

Aaron and Ethan both stood up, but Liam raised his hand.

"Just me for now."

Marcus's parents looked at him, and he shook his head.

"I'll be right back." And then he followed Liam out the door, leaving the others behind.

"I'm not going to hit you," Liam said.

"I deserve it."

"I don't know what happened between you and my sister, but Arden said that it's a communication issue. So, I'm going to believe that. Believe you're going to fix this. I don't care what you fucking need to do. But you will fix this." He held out a fisted hand, and Marcus flinched. "I said I wasn't going to hit you. Take it." Marcus held out his palm, and then Liam dropped Bristol's engagement ring in it.

"Fuck."

"Yeah. Arden did tell me a little bit. About the promise. About how you two were trying to figure things out. I don't care. I really don't. But you can and will fix this because no one's blaming you for what happened. So, you don't get to do that either."

"If I had been there, this wouldn't have happened."

"Bullshit. If any of us had been there, this wouldn't have happened. But we can't be there in each other's lives twenty-four hours a day. Colin is the one to blame for this. No matter what happens, this was Colin's fault. But when she wakes up and when she's better? You need to be her best friend again. Because you are the best thing that's ever happened to her, so don't fuck this up."

"I don't know. I just need her to be healthy first."

"Damn straight. But that ring in your hand? That's a promise that means something. You gave it to her, figure out what exactly that means, and remember that you're part of this family, too. Don't fuck it up."

And then Liam left him alone, and Marcus stood there, wondering what the hell he was going to do.

"Come on inside," Aaron said from the door.

"Is she okay?" Marcus asked, turning on his heel.

"I think the doctor's going to come out soon. They're all moving around out there. I don't want you to miss anything."

"Jesus."

"Yeah, I'm going to just keep on cursing right along with you. I need my baby sister to be safe."

"I thought you were the baby," Marcus said, trying to laugh, using the old joke, but there was nothing funny about it.

"She's still our baby sister," Aaron warned and then walked back into the room, Marcus on his heels.

They waited for another thirty minutes, and then the doctor was there, letting them know that Bristol would be fine, that she'd wake soon. She'd lost a lot of blood but would recover fully.

Marcus's knees went weak, and he almost threw up, but then the others were talking, tears flowing.

Once she got moved to a different room, others would visit her. They would make sure she was safe, but Marcus knew he couldn't see her. Not yet.

Because if he saw her without that vivid life in her eyes, on her face, he didn't know what he'd do.

And before he spoke to her, before he could apologize, he needed to figure out exactly how to fix things between them.

Because he had nearly lost her, in more ways than one. He had almost lost the light and love of his life.

And he needed to figure out exactly how the fuck to fix that.

CHAPTER 20

"I'm honestly really surprised that you got the Montgomery brothers to actually leave you alone," Zia said from the other side of the couch.

Bristol smiled, and though she truly felt that grin, it didn't quite reach her eyes. At least that's what she figured from the way Zia looked at her.

"Considering that I slept most of the time they were here, and you're the one who got them to leave, I don't know why you're so surprised," Bristol said, grinning.

She had been attacked a week ago, and was now at home, resting and healing. She wasn't a hundred percent, and it would be a while before she got there, but she didn't have to stay in the hospital, and was allowed to sleep in her own bed. That was when she knew she would be okay.

Her brothers had taken turns staying the night. Her mother had taken over her guestroom completely. Tonight, however, it was only Zia at her place, thankfully.

Everyone else had taken their turns, but Zia had promised that she would take care of Bristol, even though Bristol was doing just fine on her own. Yes, her side hurt, and every time she moved, she felt like her stitches or staples were going to break or pop. That wasn't the case, but she couldn't help her overactive imagination.

And she hadn't wanted to stay away from her home.

She had bled out on her tile, and after the police had left and had taken away all of their crime scene stuff, Arden and the girls had scrubbed her kitchen from top to bottom. It gleamed, far cleaner than it had been before everything had happened.

And they'd change the locks on her doors, even though that hadn't been the issue.

They scrubbed everything and added flowers and baked goods and tons of pre-cooked meals for the freezer.

They made it so her home felt like hers, at least mostly. It was going to take a while for her to be able to breathe again without looking out to where Colin had attacked her. She refused to allow her home to only be about what Colin had done.

Her music room/studio was exactly how it had always

been. She was going to create there again. It might take a while, but she would make it happen.

There hadn't been a speck of blood on the carpet, and she might still have to go and change that one day. Add new paint to the walls, do something to make it a little bit different from what Colin had changed it into.

Yes, that was all on him. She wasn't going to blame herself for it—or maybe she had to.

She had been the one to let him in, after all.

"Hey, you are blaming yourself again, aren't you? I can see it in your face."

Bristol's brows rose. "You cannot blame me for that," Bristol said, "You can't look into my eyes and see that."

"I so can. You're either thinking about Marcus, or you're blaming yourself for what Colin did. Don't make me hit you."

"You can't hit me. I'm hurting."

"You took your pain pills. You're feeling fine. And I will hit you. Out of love."

"You're making me miss my big brothers."

"Hey, that was just cruel."

"I could be crueler and ask you why you're here rather than back in London," Bristol said, broaching the subject that both of them had done their best to ignore.

Zia shook her head.

"There's nothing to talk about there. I'm no longer with my ex, and now I'm moving back to America. I'm going to be fine. Living in Boulder. Maybe, one day, I'll settle down with a nice person, and the world will have to deal with the fact that I'm amazing."

"We always have to deal with the fact that you're amazing."

Zia grinned.

"That's wonderful, thank you. Now, we're done talking about me. What's up with you?"

"Nothing's up with me. The tour's been postponed mostly because I think they're trying to give me space, that and make sure they cut ties with Colin completely."

"He's going to jail for a very long time."

"Unless he uses that insanity plea."

"He's not going to get away with it. He knew exactly what the fuck he was doing. The jackoff."

"Yeah, there's enough evidence to put him away for a long time. And, probably here, rather than back in England."

"I don't know about the justice system or how any of that works, but as long as he's away from you, and away from any adoring fans that miss him and his beautiful art and music, that's all that matters."

"I cannot believe how many people are trashing me because of it."

"I can. Rabid fans who want to see their darlings. They're going to blame anyone they can for their favorite's mistakes."

"Still, though, the response from the people who are on my side is nice. I'm glad that we stopped them from sending flowers and things to my house."

"Yes, having them send donations to a local women's shelter was the best idea, even if they only wanted to help you out in some cases."

"I know the media isn't going to die down anytime soon. But I'm glad that I'm in a gated community, and my neighbors are kind."

It was a single gate, and she lived in the middle of it, not in some fancy neighborhood, but it had kept the media out for the time being. She didn't know how long it would last, but hopefully, the news would die down, and no one would want to talk with Bristol Montgomery about the attack anymore.

Colin's name was splashed all over the papers—photos of them from ten years ago until recently, laughing and holding one another or even playing together. Evidence of their past was all over the internet.

Everyone wanted to know about the tragic fairy tale that was this damn relationship.

No one really got it through their thick skulls that it wasn't about romance; it was about obsession and need. And it had nothing to do with her.

Thankfully, no one had really looked too deeply beneath the surface yet, and Marcus's name hadn't been put in the papers.

But she knew that would come, and they would have to deal with it when it did.

She looked down at her phone, willing it to ring. But it wouldn't.

He had texted her every day to make sure she was okay, checking in on her, but still giving her space.

She hated it.

She wanted him to be here. She wanted to tell him what she felt, wanted to know what he was feeling. She understood the need to give each other space. Right this very moment was the only time she had been in a room with a single person since the attack, and she had woken up in the hospital, dazed and calling for Marcus.

Her brothers had been there, telling her that Marcus had been in the waiting room, along with his parents, and had waited to hear that she was okay and was waking up before he left, giving her family the short time period that they had in the room with her.

He still hadn't been by the house. And she couldn't blame him for that. Things were complicated, and she didn't even know if her brothers would let him in. They had been overprotective to the point where no one was allowed in, not even her agent or her manager.

Everyone was allowed to call her or text, but even Liam had stepped in and taken calls for her.

And while she had appreciated that, she kind of

needed to do it on her own, as well. The Montgomerys, however, were known for being overprotective.

And she was a bit grateful for the time to think.

However, she missed her best friend. And she really wanted him back.

In her heart, in her soul, with her.

"Thinking about him again?" Zia said, her voice soft.

Bristol looked up at her friend and smiled softly. "Yeah, I guess I am. Why isn't he here?" she asked, the words out of her mouth before she'd even thought about it.

Zia shrugged. "I think he's giving you space and time to heal."

"I could do that with him here."

"Could you? Could you have truly figured out exactly what you needed and heal your heart and your body while stressing out and wondering what was going on between you?"

"That's stupid. I'm stressing out now, wanting him here. Before this happened, he would've been the first person by my side, holding my hand."

"Maybe. But it did happen. And you guys are in a different place now. Even though you said you didn't want that, you are. And you have to face that."

"But why isn't he here?"

"He didn't cut off communication completely. He didn't leave you in the lurch. He's giving you the time and space you need to heal, as I said. He's not making this about himself. And I admire that."

"Seriously?"

"Yes. Because you need to make sure you know exactly what you want before you give in to your next temptation with him."

"I don't know what I want."

"Exactly. So, figure it out. Figure out exactly how you're going to tell him you love him from the bottom of your heart. That way, you can both fall for each other, and everything will be fine."

"I wish I could believe that."

"I have to believe in happily ever afters. I have to believe in your happily ever after. Because if I don't? Well, then I don't really like my chances at all. And I'm quite self-centered, making this all about me."

"There's nothing self-centered about you, Zia."

"That's not what I hear," she mumbled, but then gave Bristol a look, and Bristol didn't comment on it. Zia needed time, and frankly, the other woman was right. Bristol needed hers, as well.

Bristol fell asleep soon after, needing time to heal, and she woke up a couple of hours later with Zia tucking her in and brushing her hair back from her face.

"Hey, sleepyhead, your blanket fell. I was just fixing it. And..." Zia trailed off.

"And what?"

"Your phone went off when you were sleeping."

Bristol sat up and winced. "Ouch. I keep forgetting."

"Yes, don't pop a stitch, or your mother will actually murder me."

"Sorry."

"Don't say sorry to me about hurting. However, as I said before, your phone went off, and I answered it."

"It was Marcus, wasn't it?"

"Yes, and he'll be here any minute now."

Bristol froze. "And I look like this?"

"You wanted him by your side before, and you looked worse. I can do your makeup right quick, but he has seen you in every way possible. And you know I love wearing makeup. It's art, it's a part of me, but sometimes, it's armor. It's a shield. And if that's what you need, I will help you. But I think you need to see him exactly as you are. Because that's been the problem this whole time. You've hidden part of yourself, and you shouldn't do that anymore."

"Sometimes, you're far too wise and sage for your young age."

"And, sometimes, you make me believe that."

Zia leaned down and brushed a kiss over Bristol's lips. Bristol blinked, looking at her friend.

"What was that for?"

"You scared me so much. I know your family all said this before, but you're never allowed to do that again.

You're never allowed to almost leave us. Because I love you. No, not in the way that you are finally going to tell the love of your life, but I do love you. And I need you in my life. I'm a horribly selfish person who wants you to be healthy and whole merely for my own needs, and I'm fine with that. Because then you'll still be here. Okay? So, figure out exactly what it is you want to say to Marcus so he knows how you feel. Don't hide anymore. You're both worth far more than that." And then she kissed Bristol on the lips again, leaving Bristol shocked, and sitting there in silence.

"I have no idea what to say to any of that," Bristol said honestly.

"You do not have to say anything. Just know that you are loved." The doorbell rang, and Zia grinned.

"And, this fairy tale ending will now occur."

"Life isn't all fairy tales. You and I both know that more than most."

"I do. Now, make him work for it, and make sure he knows exactly what you want and who you are. Period. If not, I'll have to beat him up."

"Zia."

"Okay, I'll mock him. But in a loving way, of course. Be good. And be you." Then Zia went to the door, opened it, and Bristol's heart stopped.

There was Marcus, wearing a zipped-up leather jacket, jeans and old boots. His face looked drawn as if he hadn't been sleeping, and she wanted to reach out and hold him, tell him he was okay.

He had to be okay, but was she okay? She was scared. He was here, after a week of not having him, he was finally here. And it felt like a lifetime ago that he'd been here last.

Why did it feel like a year since she'd seen him, rather than only days?

Why couldn't she say anything?

Zia spoke to him, and Marcus lowered his head, nodding tightly, before Zia left, waving over her shoulder and leaving her and Marcus alone in her home.

Bristol swallowed hard and looked up at him, trying to think of words. Nothing came.

He stood there, stoic, beautiful, the man she wanted to be hers. She didn't know what to say. And since that was so unlike her, she just sat there and hoped she could find the words.

"Marcus," she whispered.

"Hey. I tried to give you space. Then I realized that maybe giving you space wasn't the right thing. I don't like not knowing what to do when it comes to you. It's something that I'm not used to, and something I want to fix. So, I'm here now, and I hope you'll let me stay if only to talk to you for a minute."

"Come in. I would get up, but I'm still a little tired."

His jaw tightened, and she knew she had probably

said the wrong thing, but she couldn't take it back. She *was* tired. And she had almost died in her own home.

Getting over that was going to take time, and probably a lot of therapy. But first, there was Marcus and her, the only steady thing she'd ever had in her life, and she had to fight to keep it.

"Come closer, really," she whispered.

And then Marcus was there, sitting on the coffee table in front of her, looking at her. He didn't reach out, didn't touch her, and the distance left her feeling bereft.

"I missed you," she whispered, finally being honest with herself. With him.

"I miss you so fucking much. I shouldn't have walked out that day, shouldn't have walked out ever."

"No, you don't get to blame yourself for what happened."

His brows rose. "I might, a little bit. Mostly because I can't hurt Colin."

"He's gone. We never have to worry about him again. I promise."

"I need to be the one making the promises," Marcus whispered, leaning forward.

"Maybe, or maybe we need to make them together."

Marcus let out a breath and rubbed his hand over his face.

"I guess we should start at the beginning?" he asked, and Bristol nodded.

"I'm going to tell you exactly how I feel," Marcus said. "Something I should've done a long fucking time ago. Because I didn't, I hurt us both."

"I'm going to say the same. So much the fucking same. Because it's not just you."

"Yeah? Are you sure you're up to this? I don't want to put too much strain on you."

"I promise, I'm not frail. I'm not going to break." A tear slid down her cheek, and Marcus reached out and rubbed it away with his thumb. "I'm not going to break," she whispered again.

"When you came up with that deal ten years ago, I thought it was insane, but I said yes right away. Do you know why?" Marcus asked, and she swallowed hard.

"Why?"

"Because I couldn't think of a world without you in it with me. You were always there, and we both did so good about not crossing those lines. I never crossed those boundaries because I didn't want to scare you away, and I didn't want to lose you. So, I figured if I had you in my life in any way possible, it would be good enough. And I didn't let myself worry about my feelings, I buried them so deep that they *couldn't* matter. But they were always there. Hiding. Waiting."

Hope sprang up in her chest, and she blinked hard. "Really?"

"Bristol, I fucking love you. And not only as friends,

though yes, that's part of it. I'm going to love you as a friend and as a person and just the amazing human being that you are for always. But I'm also in love with you. I don't know when I fell, probably long before I allowed myself to even think about it. But I fucking love you. And I don't want to lose you. Ever. Fucking ever. Do you get that? You are my everything. And I should have told you long before I walked out. But I was so fucking scared that I didn't let myself think. I left because I didn't want to hurt you, and I ended up hurting you more than I ever thought possible. Forgive me. Forgive me for not telling you how I felt because I was scared. Forgive me for not telling you that I love you."

Tears were freely falling down her cheeks at that point, and she leaned forward enough that she wasn't hurting. Marcus closed the few inches still separating them so she could put her hands on his face.

"I want to say ditto, but that would be way too easy on me."

Marcus chuckled softly, and she let out a rough laugh of her own.

"I made the promise because I was so afraid of losing you, I didn't allow myself to think about what that loss would mean. But I love you, too, Marcus. I've loved you for as long as I can remember. Though I didn't realize it was the big L until it was too late. But I want you in my life. I want to be in yours. I want to date you, and I want to marry you. I want it all. And if we have to start from scratch and figure out exactly what we are to each other while we love each other, I'm fine with that, too. Or if you want to go to Vegas right now, or maybe once I'm actually capable of standing for longer than ten minutes, then I will do that, too. Because I love you. And I'm sorry I never said it before. I really, really should have said it before."

Marcus looked at her then and smiled so widely that it hit her straight in the heart.

"For two people who know each other inside and out, we really fucking suck at this."

She laughed and leaned forward as much as she could, but then he was there, kneeling in front of the couch, holding her close, his lips a bare inch from hers.

"I don't want to be bad at this again, Bristol. So, yes, I want to marry you. I want us to be the Montgomery-Stearns and have babies and watch our families grow larger with us. I want all of that. But first, I want you to be my girlfriend, I want that label. And I want you to be my fiancée. I want that label, too. And then I want you to be my wife. Because, throughout it all, you're my best friend, Bristol Montgomery. And I will love you until the end of time. Until the end of everything."

And then his lips were on hers, and Bristol was crying, leaning into the man she loved, the man she had always loved.

She had almost lost him because she had been too afraid to lose him. The irony of that was startling.

But as he held her, and as she told him more about how she was feeling, what she was thinking, she knew they would get through this. They would come out stronger than ever.

Because Bristol Montgomery had fallen for her best friend.

And in the best way possible, he had fallen for her back.

And that was exactly the promise they had made before, and the one they would keep forever.

EPILOGUE

ile floor under his knees probably wasn't good for Marcus, but he didn't fucking care. He had Bristol's leg over his shoulder, and his mouth on her pussy, the shower feeling a little too small. But he was fine. He'd make this work. Watching the love of his life come on his face? Totally worth any aches and pains.

He lapped at her pussy, licking, sucking on her clit, and when her legs shook around him, and he knew she was coming, he moved to his feet and plunged inside of her, filling her with one stroke, leaving both of them breathless.

"Dear, God. Can't. Breathe."

Marcus was careful around her scar, knowing that while she might be healed, he would never do anything to hurt her. Never again. Never fucking again.

She had one leg firmly on the shower floor, the other around his hip. "Ready for me to move, babe?"

"If you don't move, I'm going to have to start moving against you, and we know I don't have the best rhythm."

He laughed, wondering how the fuck he was laughing during the best sex of his life, but then he figured it was just Bristol. His Bristol.

He slid in and out of her, his thumb on her clit, the other on her hip as they both rocked into one another, the shower growing cool.

They were wasting water. He cursed, reaching out to turn off the taps before plunging into her again. They kept moving, breathing as one, panting, and then she was coming, and he was following her. Both of them shook, their mouths on each other, their hands running over slick skin as they felt every inch of one another.

And when he could breathe again, he opened his eyes and looked down at her.

"Well, that's one way to wake up."

"Yeah, and we're totally going to be late, considering I woke up with your mouth on my pussy in bed."

Marcus grinned and stroked in and out of her even though he was softening. "I can't help it. I needed my breakfast."

"If you tell me the only thing I need for breakfast is a protein shake, I'm going to hurt you."

"That was yesterday. Waking up with your mouth on my dick is pretty much the best way to rise." He winked.

"I thought last week when you woke up with me riding your dick was even better."

Marcus grinned, still stroking into her as he reached out to turn the water on again so they could finish their shower.

"That is smart. Now, no more wasting water. We need to get better at that."

"Yes, that means no more showers together."

"You're no fun," Marcus said, kissing her softly. But she laughed, pushing him away, and then they quickly washed off, mostly because they actually were late for the Montgomery lunch.

Aaron had just sold a huge piece, and they were celebrating it, and there was another excuse for the Montgomerys to get together.

He knew the family had been through a lot recently, like his family had been, so they were going to do a huge family meal. And that included all of Arden's brothers, Lincoln's cousin, and Marcus's family, as well.

He had no idea how Bristol's mom did it all, but he knew that she was going to have it catered. There would be tons of food and loads of happiness.

Exactly what he needed.

They dressed quickly, both of them laughing as they

went through the schedule for their upcoming week. He knew that she would be going on tour soon now that she was healed, and since his big project was over, he was working on the setup for the next big grant.

They were making it work, somehow.

His career path kept him home mostly, while hers would keep her far away from him in some cases. But there were ways around that, and both of them had dreams and lives that they wanted to fulfill and live, so they were working it out.

And she wore his ring, something he would never forget.

They were taking it slow, to the point where the wedding wouldn't be until after the others got married.

But she wanted his ring, and he wanted to see it on her.

And that meant they would assume all the labels at once, but they were at least aware of it this time.

He would ask her how she felt, and he would tell her what he was feeling.

It wasn't something he was really good at usually, but he was getting better.

By the time that they got to Bristol's family's house, they were the last ones to arrive, but he'd known that would happen. He couldn't help it after waking up with Bristol right there, all naked and ready.

"Don't look at me like that, my mother and father are going to know exactly what you did to me."

"Then you can't look at me like that either. My parents and my sisters are in there. Waiting. Watching."

"What are you guys hiding?" Aaron asked, leaning against the doorjamb.

"Nothing," Bristol said quickly. She went up to her toes and kissed Aaron on the cheek. "I'm so happy for you. Look at my baby brother. Doing amazing in the art world and selling pieces to royalty."

"I'm doing an art show, too. Look at me. Being all art-like."

"You're a dork. But I love you."

"I am a dork. But I can't help it. It's just who I am."

"That is true," she said, and then went to kiss his other cheek.

Marcus held out a hand, and Aaron shook it and grinned.

"Good to see you're taking care of my baby sister."

"You're the baby," Bristol corrected.

"Whatever," Aaron said.

They made their way inside and said hello to everybody, the noise getting louder with each passing moment. There were so many people there, so many the Montgomerys had claimed as their family. Marcus had felt that he was a part of the family since he was a kid, and now he was going to be related in truth, something his parents were very excited about.

"I can't wait for you to make little babies," his mother said from his side, and Marcus choked on his drink.

"Could you say that any louder, Mom?"

"I could. But then that would embarrass poor Bristol, and I don't want to embarrass her."

"Just me, then?"

"Of course, you're my baby boy."

"I swear, moms sure do love calling us babies," Aaron said, coming up to them.

"You know, you are the last single Montgomery," Marcus's mother said solemnly.

Aaron shrugged, though there was something in his eye that Marcus couldn't quite decipher. "Someone does have to hold out."

Mrs. Montgomery leaned forward. "I'm sure that's the case. But if you're not careful, all of us will start matchmaking. We want you to be happy, and that means you may have to deal with it."

Aaron's face turned ashen. "I don't need matchmaking. I can find my own matches."

"Can you?" Marcus's mom asked all innocently, and Marcus laughed out loud.

"Well, you've done it now. My mother's going to find you someone if you're not careful."

"I'll help," Mrs. Montgomery said, her eyes twinkling.

"Dear God. Let's not do that. No matchmaking."

"Oh, can I help, too?" Bristol asked, coming up to his side. Marcus leaned down and kissed the top of her head, and she sighed into him. He didn't miss the look that the two mothers gave each other, each grinning wildly, but he didn't mind it.

They had always been close, and now they were even closer because of him and Bristol.

Somehow, the fates had been kind to him and had given him his happily ever after far earlier than he would've guessed. He had been far too stubborn to realize it until he'd almost lost it all.

But now he had the love of his life in his arms, the loudest family full of so much that he could barely stand it, and a future that seemed pretty damn good.

All it had taken was finally saying the words that he should have long ago.

"Love you, Bristol."

She looked up at him, her eyes wide. "I love you, too, Marcus."

She was his best friend, his future, and the one person that he knew he could finally tell everything to.

He was so fucking happy that he had met the Montgomerys.

THE END

Next in the Montgomery Ink: Boulder series?
It's Aaron's turn in SEDUCED IN INK.

**WANT TO READ A SPECIAL BONUS EPILOGUE
FEATURING BRISTOL & MARCUS? CLICK HERE!**

A NOTE FROM CARRIE ANN RYAN

Thank you so much for reading **EMBRACED IN INK**. I do hope if you liked this story, that you would please leave a review! Reviews help authors *and* readers.

Bristol and Marcus were so romantic. I love that they knew what they wanted even if they told themselves they didn't.

Up next is Aaron and Madison! These two are already a little headstrong and unconventional. I can't wait to show you what they are up to.

There are also a few side characters in this romance that are begging for a story...hmm...I do believe I might have to listen to them!

And if you're new to my books, you can start anywhere within the my interconnected series and catch up! Each book is a stand alone, so jump around!

Don't miss out on the Montgomery Ink World!

- Montgomery Ink (The Denver Montgomerys)
- Montgomery Ink: Colorado Springs (The Colorado Springs Montgomery Cousins)
- Montgomery Ink: Boulder (The Boulder Montgomery Cousins)
- Gallagher Brothers (Jake's Brothers from Ink Enduring)
- Whiskey and Lies (Tabby's Brothers from Ink Exposed)
- Fractured Connections (Mace's sisters from Fallen Ink)
- Less Than (Dimitri's siblings from Restless Ink)
- Promise Me (Arden's siblings from Wrapped in Ink)

If you want to make sure you know what's coming next from me, you can sign up for my newsletter at www. CarrieAnnRyan.com; follow me on twitter at @Carrie-AnnRyan, or like my Facebook page. I also have a Facebook Fan Club where we have trivia, chats, and other goodies. You guys are the reason I get to do what I do and I thank you.

Make sure you're signed up for my MAILING LIST so you can know when the next releases are available as well as find giveaways and FREE READS.

Happy Reading!

The Montgomery Ink: Boulder Series:
Book 1: Wrapped in Ink
Book 2: Sated in Ink
Book 3: Embraced in Ink
Book 4: Seduced in Ink
Book 4.5: Captured in Ink

WANT TO READ A SPECIAL **BONUS EPILOGUE** FEATURING **BRISTOL & MARCUS? CLICK HERE!**

Want to keep up to date with the next Carrie Ann Ryan Release? Receive Text Alerts easily!
Text CARRIE to 210-741-8720

ABOUT THE AUTHOR

Carrie Ann Ryan is the New York Times and USA Today bestselling author of contemporary, paranormal, and young adult romance. Her works include the Montgomery Ink, Redwood Pack, Fractured Connections, and Elements of Five series, which have sold over 3.0 million books worldwide. She started writing while in graduate school for her advanced degree in chemistry and hasn't stopped since. Carrie Ann has written over seventy-five novels and novellas with more in the works. When she's not losing herself in her emotional and action-packed worlds, she's reading as much as she can while wrangling her clowder of cats who have more followers than she does.

www.CarrieAnnRyan.com

ALSO FROM CARRIE ANN RYAN

The Montgomery Ink: Boulder Series:
Book 1: Wrapped in Ink
Book 2: Sated in Ink
Book 3: Embraced in Ink
Book 4: Seduced in Ink
Book 4.5: Captured in Ink

The Montgomery Ink: Fort Collins Series:
Book 1: Inked Persuasion

The Less Than Series:
Book 1: Breathless With Her
Book 2: Reckless With You
Book 3: Shameless With Him

The Elements of Five Series:
    Book 1: From Breath and Ruin
    Book 2: From Flame and Ash
    Book 3: From Spirit and Binding

The Promise Me Series:
    Book 1: Forever Only Once
    Book 2: From That Moment
    Book 3: Far From Destined
    Book 4: From Our First

The Fractured Connections Series:
    Book 1: Breaking Without You
    Book 2: Shouldn't Have You
    Book 3: Falling With You
    Book 4: Taken With You

Montgomery Ink: Colorado Springs
    Book 1: Fallen Ink
    Book 2: Restless Ink
    Book 2.5: Ashes to Ink
    Book 3: Jagged Ink
    Book 3.5: Ink by Numbers

Montgomery Ink:
    Book 0.5: Ink Inspired

Book 0.6: Ink Reunited
Book 1: Delicate Ink
Book 1.5: Forever Ink
Book 2: Tempting Boundaries
Book 3: Harder than Words
Book 4: Written in Ink
Book 4.5: Hidden Ink
Book 5: Ink Enduring
Book 6: Ink Exposed
Book 6.5: Adoring Ink
Book 6.6: Love, Honor, & Ink
Book 7: Inked Expressions
Book 7.3: Dropout
Book 7.5: Executive Ink
Book 8: Inked Memories
Book 8.5: Inked Nights
Book 8.7: Second Chance Ink

The Gallagher Brothers Series:
Book 1: Love Restored
Book 2: Passion Restored
Book 3: Hope Restored

The Whiskey and Lies Series:
Book 1: Whiskey Secrets
Book 2: Whiskey Reveals

Book 3: Whiskey Undone

The Talon Pack:
Book 1: Tattered Loyalties
Book 2: An Alpha's Choice
Book 3: Mated in Mist
Book 4: Wolf Betrayed
Book 5: Fractured Silence
Book 6: Destiny Disgraced
Book 7: Eternal Mourning
Book 8: Strength Enduring
Book 9: Forever Broken

Redwood Pack Series:
Book 1: An Alpha's Path
Book 2: A Taste for a Mate
Book 3: Trinity Bound
Book 3.5: A Night Away
Book 4: Enforcer's Redemption
Book 4.5: Blurred Expectations
Book 4.7: Forgiveness
Book 5: Shattered Emotions
Book 6: Hidden Destiny
Book 6.5: A Beta's Haven
Book 7: Fighting Fate
Book 7.5: Loving the Omega

Book 7.7: The Hunted Heart

Book 8: Wicked Wolf

The Branded Pack Series:

(Written with Alexandra Ivy)

Book 1: Stolen and Forgiven

Book 2: Abandoned and Unseen

Book 3: Buried and Shadowed

Dante's Circle Series:

Book 1: Dust of My Wings

Book 2: Her Warriors' Three Wishes

Book 3: An Unlucky Moon

Book 3.5: His Choice

Book 4: Tangled Innocence

Book 5: Fierce Enchantment

Book 6: An Immortal's Song

Book 7: Prowled Darkness

Book 8: Dante's Circle Reborn

Holiday, Montana Series:

Book 1: Charmed Spirits

Book 2: Santa's Executive

Book 3: Finding Abigail

Book 4: Her Lucky Love

Book 5: Dreams of Ivory

ALSO FROM CARRIE ANN RYAN

The Happy Ever After Series:
Flame and Ink
Ink Ever After

Single Title:
Finally Found You